MURDER IN THE SOUTH OF FRANCE

An addictive crime mystery full of twists

ROY LEWIS

Arnold Landon Mysteries Book 18

Originally published as *Headhunter*

Revised edition 2022
Joffe Books, London
www.joffebooks.com

First published in Great Britain in 2002
as *Headhunter*

This paperback edition was first published
in Great Britain in 2022

ISBN: 978-1-80405-366-9

NOTE TO THE READER

Please note this book is set in the early 2000s in England, a time before ubiquitous CCTV, and when social attitudes were very different.

PROLOGUE

He didn't feel like a killer.

He remembered the explosion of rage, the battering, the bitterness and anger that had driven him. He stared at his knuckles, the skin still raw and marked with half-healed scars, and he remembered the way the blood had flown, staining the shirt he had later burned in self-disgust. But he looked up at the sky, bright blue, cloud-flecked, and in spite of the viciousness, and the rage, and even the surge of almost sexual excitement he had felt at the pounding he had delivered to the face, he still didn't feel like a killer.

Slowly he walked along the riverside in the lengthening afternoon shadows, shambling past the expensive high-rise development of flats that had replaced the old cottages along Dolphin Quays. The previous weekend there had been a public concert on the quay but the temporary stands had now been taken down and the Fish Quay at North Shields was almost deserted: scattered newspapers scuttled along in the whipping sea breezes as an elderly couple sat eating fish and chips on a bench on the quayside, watching some children chasing the squawking seagulls scavenging for scraps on the wooden baulks at the water's edge. A single rusting trawler lay alongside the dock with its dilapidated sheds, evidence of the long declining fishing industry on the Tyne, but he trudged past carelessly, head down, angry visions still exploding in his head, red and black and violent.

He crossed the quay and headed for the broad curving swathe of the promenade that stretched from North Shields to Tynemouth. He was hardly aware of the gleaming white ferry that came sidling into the river, returning from Bergen, preceded fussily by the pilot boat negotiating the swing of the river. As the afternoon sun glinted on the black waves rippling towards the banks he walked slowly, his mind in turmoil. The river widened to his right and the long stretch of the sea opened out ahead of him. To his left was the headland dominated by the statue to Admiral Collingwood gazing out towards the sandy beach at South Shields. Beyond the statue were the stark ruins of the ancient abbey, blank crumbling walls facing the dark waters of the North Sea.

The sun was hot on the back of his neck, quarrelling gulls swirled above his head and suddenly he felt dizzy, He stopped, sat down on a bench on the deserted promenade. In front of him was the stretch of the river known as the Black Rocks, sharp-toothed edges exposed now at low tide and picked over by wading birds. Craggy and dangerous, the rocks had been the cause of many a disaster in the days when the proud three-masters had dominated the river, carrying coal and iron, silk and rubber, crossing the North Sea to distant places like Eskimo Point, Cape Town or Karachi. Now the menacing rocks were passed with indifference by the piloted ferry, slipping up river along the narrow channel of the Port of Tyne. Like the men on the ferry, he barely noticed them. His swollen knuckles throbbed and ached, but his thoughts pained him more. He didn't feel like a killer and yet the rage that had been within him, the savagery he had experienced . . .

A commotion of black-feathered birds swirled high in front of him, screeching their displeasure at something happening below him, and he became vaguely aware that there were three boys clambering over the black rocks beyond the promenade rail. They were doing the aimless things that young boys always did at the water's edge, the kind of things he had himself done years ago: scrambling over rocks, fishing in inviting pools, daring slippery surfaces, tasting of danger at the edge of the black river surge from the wake of the passing ferry. He watched them with dulled eyes, wondering vaguely why they were not at school.

The thought was momentary only: the blackness came back. He leaned forward, put his throbbing head in his hands and tried to dispel the memory of blood and rage. He sat there silently as the sun beat on the back of his neck and the time slipped past unheeded.

'Hey, mister!'

His eyes were closed, red stars exploding in the darkness.

'Hey, *mister!*'

He looked up reluctantly, blinking in the afternoon sunlight. The tallest of the three boys was standing precariously on a black rock, some fifty yards from him. The other two were huddled together, staring at a dark, gleaming mass that they seemed to have dragged from among the rocks. Perhaps they had found a dead seal, or a large fish.

'Mister! You better come here!'

The tone was arrogant, peremptory and yet it held a quavering edge, a hint of youthful fear and uncertainty. The boy was waving, the others still staring at the thing in front of them. Slowly, reluctantly he got to his feet. He looked around, there was no one else on the promenade. He hesitated, and then as the boy waved again he ducked his head, climbed under the rusting barrier rail and gingerly lowered himself down from the promenade wall, dropping awkwardly on to the shiny rocks below. Holding his balance with difficulty he scrambled across the slippery rocks towards the gesticulating boy. When he reached the small group they drew more tightly together, as though uncertain: the boy who had called him gestured towards the gleaming black material.

'Saw it caught on the rocks. Dragged it in. But there's a funny smell to it.'

3

The odour was strong. It caught in the back of his throat as he leaned over it. The smell of brine, seaweed, but sweet and sickly in addition. He almost slipped and fell as he stepped past the huddled boys, inspecting what seemed to be a large, black, heavy duty plastic bundle, and something in his stomach dropped. His mind had been full of memory and blood and violence and he knew that it was all part of the same thing: what lay at his feet meant trouble and savagery. His hand trembled as he knelt on the slippery rock, stretched out and seized the edge of the plastic. The bundle was heavy. He dragged at it and the thing turned, the hard, rough edge of the stiff plastic scratching at the back of his hand so that he swore at the sudden pain in his already lacerated hand. As he dragged it across the rock the plastic ripped, and he saw something inside. His stomach churned. He stood up, his worst nightmare coming alive. Gagging, he turned to the boys.

'Why aren't you at school?'

'What's it to you, mister?' The tallest boy was defiant. 'Hey, you know what's in that bundle?'

'You better get the hell out of here. Go on, get off the beach.'

They stood there, the biggest boy defiant, hands on hips, unwilling to respond to him, curious about the thing at his feet.

'*Get off the beach!*'

He snarled the words, and there was something in his tone that made the boys back off. The smallest started to clamber back towards the promenade. Reluctantly, the other two followed him.

'What you going to do with that thing?' the tallest boy shouted from a distance. 'It was us who found it, remember!' Then he turned and clambered after his companions, climbing up to the promenade rail. 'It was us who found it!' There was a complaining whine to his tone. They stood there for a few moments on the promenade, muttering amongst themselves and then, dragging their feet, kicking occasionally at the

4

rails, they slowly walked towards the Fish Quay, arguing and gesticulating, looking back at him with disgusted frustration.

The bundle lay at his feet. He could not think clearly, had no idea what to do next. His mind was still in turmoil, his head ached. The smell of death was still in his nostrils.

He stood there, staring at the torn black plastic bundle lying on the rocks for what seemed an age. At last he shook himself and turned, made his way back towards the railed promenade, clumsy, feet slipping on the slimy, seaweed-covered rocks. He hauled himself up with difficulty, his senses dulled as he walked back towards the Fish Quay.

He stood outside the telephone box for several minutes. He was vaguely aware there was someone watching him. He turned his head, saw the huddle of boys, curious still. He entered the box, took a deep breath, and with a trembling, reluctant finger dialled the emergency number.

It was a mistake. He knew in his bones it was a mistake after what he had done. But he didn't feel like a killer . . .

* * *

Twelve hours later and twelve miles away the four men in the unmarked police van sat silently, tension building in their veins. They all knew the drill. They each knew what they had to do. Detective Sergeant Robinson savoured the sting of tobacco on his tongue. A broad-shouldered, shaggy-haired man of thirty-eight, he was the leader of the group. Tobacco calmed the inevitable twisting of the stomach muscles as he waited to give the order. He took one last drag at his cigarette, consulted his watch nervously: timing was essential. They were only one of eight groups scattered around the north-east — Newcastle, Durham, Middlesbrough, Morpeth, Alnwick — and movements had to be closely co-ordinated. In a dawn raid of this kind, after months of patient planning, there had to be no mistakes, no opportunity for anyone of the villains to pick up a phone, issue a warning, cover up or destroy evidence, get out of the premises before they got collared.

A second van nosed its almost noiseless way into the cul-de-sac, engine cut. Headlights flickered.

'Okay. Showtime,' Robinson grunted.

The doors of the van opened on well-oiled hinges, and the four men stepped out. They moved swiftly, linking up with the men from the other van. Their rubber-soled boots made hardly a sound as they moved into the quiet road together, one group splitting away, down the narrow lane which led to the rear of the houses. After a tense, thirty-second wait Robinson nodded, muttered the go-ahead, and the group charged up the drive of the detached house on the edge of the cul-de-sac.

It took three heavy blows of the hammer before Robinson kicked hard with his boot. When the door crashed down he was first into the hallway. Immediately, all was pandemonium: there was a confused shouting from upstairs, the squad split, two men hunting through the downstairs rooms, the others pounding up the stairs. They slammed open a bedroom door and plunged inside, dark-clothed, yelling: there was a man there in bed, mouth open, shouting silently in terror, his vocal cords unresponsive to his panic. At the other end of the corridor a door slammed. Robinson turned, ran towards the door and grabbed the doorknob. The room was locked.

He turned, and yelled at the others. The sledgehammer thundered into the door. It splintered, the hinges screamed as Robinson kicked the door inward, and they forced their way into the bedroom beyond.

The room was lit with a bluish, almost satanic glow, flickering from the monitor screen. Seated at the computer was a man dressed in a string vest and shorts. He was barefooted, middle-aged, balding and he cast one panicked glance over his shoulder before he turned back, ignored their charging presence as his pudgy fingers raced across the keyboard. Images flashed and faded across the blue screen in front of him.

Robinson rushed forward, grabbed the man by the shoulder and dragged him away from the machine. The typist chair on which the man had been sitting skidded and crashed over. The man himself fell sideways, rolling against the desk in the corner, yelling in pain. Robinson paid no attention to him, concentrating, crouched over the computer screen, touching a few keys in sequence. Then the room fell silent as a sequence of images formed on the screen.

Robinson let out a deep breath of satisfaction. This was what they had hoped for. For months they had been building a case, but what he was seeing in front of him now would be the clinching evidence. He relaxed a little, his shoulders slumping, releasing the tension. He tapped a few more keys, opened up the address book. He scrolled through it and grunted.

The pudgy man on the floor moaned. 'You got no right to do this. You've broken my arm,' he complained in a whining tone.

'A broken arm is going to be the least of your problems,' Robinson said without even glancing at him. 'We've got you, you sick bastard. You and the rest of your bloody Starlight Club.'

He closed down the computer and unplugged it. He flicked on his mobile phone. 'Operation completed successfully.'

The man on the bedroom floor moaned again. 'I could be dying here,' he complained.

Robinson ignored him. He gestured to his companions. 'Get him downstairs with the other guy.' His voice tightened with disgust. 'And don't worry too much if he screams.'

CHAPTER ONE

1

Joe Holderness looked up in exasperation at the blue, vapour-trailed sky above him and thrust his hands deep into the pockets of his donkey jacket. A burly, middle-aged man with reddish, thinning hair and a lugubrious expression, he was known to display few airs and graces in spite of his wealth. A blunt, self-made Yorkshireman, he had built up his housing business over the years with a dedication that had ruined two marriages and estranged him from his three children, but his stubbornness had made him reject any change in personality: he still wore an ancient donkey jacket, scarred boots, and a dogged, uncompromising air. He lacked sophistication and despised small talk. Arnold Landon quite liked him.

'So,' Holderness grunted, 'let's stop beating about the bush. What's the bottom line?'

It had been a year since Arnold had first visited the site at Fordbridge, above the Roman settlement and the medi-eval pack bridge. The sloping hill was windswept, with a distant view of the sea that brought a salty tang to the air when the westerlies blew. Behind them, cresting the hill was a clump of ancient beech, leaning crookedly, accommodat-ing the breezes. Arnold hesitated over his reply, but knew that prevarication would be resented by the straight-talking

Yorkshireman. 'My guess would be that it'll take at least another eight months.'

'Just because you found a flaming chariot?' Holderness grumbled belligerently.

Standing beside Arnold, Portia Tyrrel shifted her stance, stepping forward slightly into Holderness's line of sight. She held the view that most men were susceptible to female persuasion. Born in Singapore, slim and dark-haired, she possessed a striking beauty resulting from the union of a Chinese mother and a Scottish father. She had no compunction about using her femininity. Indeed she could exploit it with ruthlessness on occasions, as Arnold was well aware. She leaned forward now, smiling at Holderness.

'It's not exactly a chariot,' she demurred. 'That would suggest a military burial. But this interment is of a woman, and I think it would be more accurate to describe the burial as of a two-wheeled cart, as opposed to the four-wheeled wagons that are known from the earliest phases of the Iron Age in Europe.'

Holderness hunched his shoulders and glared at her, as unimpressed by her erudition as he was impervious to her charm. 'So you'll hold me up even further, just over a bloody cart?' he snarled.

Hastily, Arnold intervened, casting a warning glance at Portia. 'It's not too important how we describe the find. The fact is, there's been very little research done on gender in Iron Age societies, so this burial inevitably raises major questions about the role and status of women of that period. We're naturally very grateful for the way in which you've co-operated, Mr Holderness, but the more we carry on with the excavation, I'm afraid the more important the site seems to be.'

Holderness clicked his tongue impatiently. He glared around at the site. The sea-wind raised his thinning hair and he shook his head. 'First of all it's an old house—'

'A medieval manorial complex,' Portia corrected primly, slightly nettled that he paid her so little attention.

'Then it's a chariot—'

'A carriage, really, of the kind used as everyday transport for people,' Portia insisted. When Arnold shot her another warning glance, she smiled sweetly at him, refusing to be denied. 'The equivalent of a horse-drawn trap, really.'

Joe Holderness eyed her sourly. He had an old-fashioned view about the place of women in society and he was not impressed by her interventions. He scratched his stubbled cheek with cracked, grimy fingernails. 'And now, just because you've found a bunch of bits and pieces of old iron in the excavation you're telling me work on the housing estate will have to be held up for months again.'

'We're appreciative of your cooperation, Mr Holderness,' Arnold repeated.

Holderness grunted, unconvinced, shaking his head. 'I don't know I can wait that long. I got money tied up . . . Your boss, that Miss Stannard, she assured me months ago that this would be all wrapped up—'

'Miss Stannard has no crystal ball. She wasn't to know the extent of the discoveries here,' Portia Tyrrel commented with a deprecating smile that suggested Karen Stannard could sometimes be very wrong. 'But we'll be reporting to her of course, and I'm sure she'll be in touch with you again, to confirm the arrangements, and the agreements made. The agreements you've already entered into.'

The emphasis on the last words was not lost upon the grizzled property developer. His eyes narrowed. 'Agreements can be altered,' Holderness countered grimly. 'When you get back to your office, you can tell Miss Stannard that I'll be in to see her. Sooner rather than later.' He eyed Arnold suspiciously. 'Eight months, you say?'

'That would be my guess.'

'I'll give you three. After that all agreements are off. Tell that to Miss Stannard.'

Portia raised an elegant eyebrow, glanced at Arnold, shrugged and turned away. She was washing her hands of this: there was no way she would be explaining things to Karen Stannard. Arnold groaned mentally. He could guess just who would be held responsible for this particular decision by Joe Holderness.

* * *

'What the hell did you *say* to him to make him change his mind like that?' Karen Stannard demanded angrily, pacing up and down, tapping a pencil against the knuckles of her left hand.

Arnold stiffened in his chair. They were together in Karen Stannard's office: Portia sitting beside him, but a little behind him as though she was acknowledging his seniority — and his responsibility. It was one of the things the two women had in common, Arnold considered: they were each liable to hold him responsible for any problems that arose in the Department of Museums and Antiquities. It was true that he had been there longer than either of them, but Karen was head of the department and Portia worked as her assistant. Yet although his own responsibilities were clearly defined, and hedged around by Karen, it always seemed to end up with Arnold carrying the can.

'In my view Joe Holderness has been very patient,' he argued. 'When he started work on that building site at Fordbridge he was public-spirited enough to stop excavations when he came across the old walls of the medieval manor complex. It was he who informed us, after all — he could have kept quiet about the finds. And the later discovery was unexpected: it only came about when Holderness rerouted his access road, and even that was because we slapped a tree preservation order on him, because of the ancient oaks beyond the beech copse. But he is a businessman, after all: he's invested a great deal of capital in this building site, and he can't be expected to hold off forever.'

'Eight months is not for ever.' Karen snapped.

'Three months is all he would give us,' Portia said in a quiet voice, adding primly, 'after Arnold explained things to him.'

Karen Stannard glowered at Arnold. Her anger served only to emphasize her beauty. She threw the pencil down on her desk, sat down, leaned her head back on the leather executive chair she had recently acquired for her office, and stared at the ceiling. Light from the window behind her touched her hair, bringing out red-gold tints. Her classical features seemed to be set in anger, but her breathing was regular and Arnold knew her ice-cold brain would be calculating, weighing up possibilities, seeking solutions. Her slim fingers drummed lightly on the leather-topped desk in front of her, and she lowered her head, fixed Arnold with a calculating glance. As ever, he wondered about the colour of her eyes: the colour seemed to change with her mood, but he was unable to read her expression this morning.

The silence grew around them. Portia Tyrrel waited patiently, her slim body motionless in her chair, a feline waiting for the mouse to break cover. Much of this was a game to her, Arnold had long since concluded. She enjoyed teasing out reactions from both Karen and Arnold himself, playing one off against the other. But as he glanced at her he could also recall the way she had used him one summer afternoon, in the long, sweet grass, a year ago now. He could still remember the cool softness of her body, the way she had moved against him, the touch of her fingers . . .

'Right,' Karen Stannard said purposefully, leaning forward to place her elbows on the desk in front of her. 'I've had your report, Arnold, but let's go over the major points once more. The hilltop position of this burial is unusual for an Iron Age interment. You're suggesting a fourth or third century BC date.'

'That's right,' Arnold nodded hastily, feeling a stab of guilt at the way in which his thoughts had wandered. 'And the inhumation is important because it's of a mature woman. She was buried on her left side — usually such a body would be placed in the grave with the head to the north.'

'The pattern is reversed here,' Portia interrupted. Karen Stannard rewarded her with a cool glance.

14

'The woman was laid in a small hollow,' Arnold continued, 'probably on a mat, or the hide of an animal. Over the upper part of her body had been placed joints of pig—'

'Traditional fare for the journey to the underworld,' Portia added smugly.

'—and several split skulls. The dismantled carriage or chariot was placed in the grave thereafter — axle, pole, with the wheels in the northern half of the grave. We've found the yoke, rein rings, wheel stops. In the square ditch that surrounded the burial, marking the edge of a low barrow mound, we also found a few shards of pottery and more pig bones, which had eroded into the ditch from the surface of the barrow.'

Karen Stannard's brow creased in thought. 'Fine, but all this isn't really enough to argue strongly that we need another eight months to continue. Joe Holderness isn't going to be persuaded to grant us extra time by detail of this kind. He'll want something more concrete.'

'I don't think Holderness will be persuaded at all,' Arnold suggested. 'He's a dogged, dogmatic man. I think he's made a decision, and he won't budge. But an extension of the work is needed. We've made unexpected discoveries. The lynchpins and nave hoops were covered in bronze sheeting but the terrets, rein rings and strap unions are all decorated—'

'Coral studs, it would seem,' Portia offered.

'That's yet to be confirmed,' Arnold argued, a little irritated by her self-important interventions, 'and there are also red glass enamel studs which would suggest the carriage was old, well used.'

'Not specifically made for the burial, you mean?' Karen asked.

'That's right. And then there's the iron mirror, and the mass of tiny blue beads only a few millimetres across . . .' Karen nodded thoughtfully. 'But you're convinced Holderness won't budge on time.'

'That's my belief,' Arnold agreed.

'So we have to move fast.'

'We don't have the resources,' Arnold reminded her.

All three were silent for a while. Karen Stannard shook her head. 'I can't go back to the council: Powell Frinton, our revered Chief Executive, has already warned me there'll be no support for more money to support this research. And we'd draw a blank with the Heritage Council too. They'll put no more cash into any of our projects. Not while work is continuing on the sea cave up at Abbey Head.'

'My team is still active there,' Portia Tyrrel intervened, reminding them that she had been allocated responsibility for oversight of the project. 'Sketches of the engravings on the walls of the sea cave have now been completed, and are being analysed at the university. We have someone working on the weather magic shamanic meanings, and the possible rituals that would have been connected with the rain-bull depicted on the roof of the sea cave. There's a lot still to do, not least on the artefacts we've unearthed. But, well, everything is at full stretch. As Arnold says, we're short of manpower.'

'And expertise,' Karen added irritably. 'I'm well aware of the position.' She clicked her tongue in frustration, glaring at Arnold. 'I think this thing with Holderness has clearly been mishandled. I should have talked to him myself. But why it always has to be left to me . . . All right, give me some time to think about this.' The darkness of her eyes conveyed her displeasure as she glowered at Arnold. 'Get your report right up to date. I've got to show it to a few people.'

She rose to her feet and nodded. It was a dismissal.

In the corridor outside the office Portia giggled, nudged Arnold's arm conspiratorially. 'Don't you just *love* it when she gets niggled, Arnold?'

Arnold returned to his office. There was a pile of paper-work waiting there for him on his desk. He sighed. It was all a long way from the days when he had tramped the Yorkshire hills with his father, inspecting old ruins, indulging his father's passion for industrial archaeology. In the end, of course, he had drifted into this work at the Department of

Museums and Antiquities: he had no academic background, but he had been driven by an interest in ancient things, instilled in him by his father, and by the practical knowledge that had been imparted to him. And it was still a job he loved, for it gave him the opportunity to visit the high, buzzard-flown Northumbrian fells where four thousand years ago men had stripped away the trees and farmed the uplands until erosion had carved out the broad empty sweep of the moorland, purple-heathered, gorse-strewn. There were the ruined castles and pele houses to inspect, medieval complexes and traces of Viking and Roman occupation; the excavations of long-forgotten villages, the ancient mysteries of sea caves, the evidence of ritual and mind-flight, and death.

But there was also the paperwork, heaped up there in front of him, a necessary adjunct to the freedom he enjoyed on the fells, with the salty breeze in his face and the springy heather under his feet.

It was all part of the job, and now he applied himself to it.

At lunchtime he took a break and wandered down to the canteen, ordered a cup of coffee and took a seat by himself near the window overlooking the car park. He saw Portia Tyrrel emerge, dark skirt, crisp white blouse, walking across the car park to head off into town. An appointment for lunch, perhaps. He still wondered about her from time to time. There was an ambivalence about his feelings for her. She was clever, knowledgeable and beautiful, but he knew of her inner hardness, an ambitious drive that caused her to calculate the percentages in all her actions, and her relationships. A year ago, there had been a brief closeness between them on the high fell, but it had been momentary. When she had left him, he had realized that making love for her that day had been in some way the achievement of a triumph over someone she saw as a professional rival. He sighed, shaking his head as he mused. He doubted whether he would ever get to understand just what made Portia Tyrrel tick.

'*Bonjour, mon général. Comment ça va?*'

The man who slid into the seat opposite Arnold was an object of departmental dislike. His thickness of skin enabled him to ignore it, or perhaps even be unaware of it. Jerry Picton was a small man in every way: he had a mean mouth and pitted skin, he displayed prejudices which were an anathema to Arnold. He was untrustworthy, the purveyor of office gossip, and his conversations were invariably tinged with malice. He winked at Arnold now and bared stained teeth in a conspiratorial grin. 'Good place to sit, this. Watch what's going on in the car park, know what I mean? Who's doing what to whom, that sort of thing.' He bit enthusiastically into a ham-filled baguette, chomped away, transferred the half-masticated material into his bulging cheek 'So how you gettin' on these days with the witches? Hear you're in trouble again.'

'I don't think so,' Arnold replied guardedly.

'No?' Jerry Picton raised inquisitive eyebrows. 'From what I hear, you more or less cocked up the dig at Fordbridge.'

'Rumour travels fast, and gossip even faster,' Arnold replied drily.

'Oh, this was horse's mouth stuff, Arnold. Right out of the Chinese box, so to speak.' Slyly, Picton asked, 'You fancy her, Arnold?'

'Who?'

'Don't show ignorant with me.' Picton chewed away and grinned confidentially. 'Little Miss Singapore. Saw you watching her cross the car park. Nice bit of stuff, I reckon. But maybe you already know from experience . . . Though I always thought you'd eventually have a crack at Miss Stannard. Not that you'd have got anywhere, of course. Knowing her leanings, like.'

His piggy eyes were fixed on Arnold, watching for reaction. Arnold wondered whether it had actually been Picton who had started the rumours of Karen Stannard's sexual predilections when she had first arrived at the department; Picton, or disappointed Lotharios and middle-aged councillors who considered their positions entitled them to favours from the female staff. Karen had certainly had friendships with some of the women she had worked with professionally, but Arnold had never subscribed to the theories that fluttered clandestinely around the department.

'I have to get back to my desk.'

'Karen cracking the whip, hey?' Picton winked. 'Now that conjures up a picture, hey? Those long legs of hers, black leather, and a whip. Tasty . . .'

Arnold left him to his juvenile, lascivious ramblings and returned to his office. The pile of files on his desk seemed to have diminished but little. The afternoon sun was hot through the window. He left open his office door so that he could have a passage of cool air. He worked steadily for an hour or more. At last he became aware that he was being observed.

He looked up. Karen Stannard was standing in the doorway, arms folded, leaning against the door jamb. When he caught her glance, she seemed momentarily disturbed, a fleeting shadow across her dark eyes as though she had been caught out in some guilty secret. She straightened, smoothed her skirt in an uncharacteristically nervous gesture, walked into the room, took a seat across the desk from him and looked about her. She had rarely visited his office. She preferred the environment of her own room, her own stamping ground where she could remain in control. Karen Stannard, he had long ago concluded, was concerned with power. The lack of it undermined her.

'Reasonably tidy for a man,' she commented on the state of the room.

'Makes life easier.'

She glanced doubtfully at the files on his desk. 'Mmm.' She shifted in her chair, crossed one leg over the other, and he became acutely aware of the lines of her body. His mind lurched back to the night they had spent together at the hotel in Alnwick. It was a dangerous track to go down.

'You wanted to see me about something?' he blurted. She held his glance steadily, and yet there was something there, shifting deep in her eyes. She seemed ill at ease. 'Next week, I'm going to Carcassonne.'

'Conference?'

She nodded. 'That's right. I should have told you sooner. I had been thinking of taking Portia with me.'

Leaving Arnold to hold the fort. It was to be expected. He was formally her deputy, though the Chief Executive had held some doubts about whether they could work together, aware as he was of Karen's feelings of professional rivalry. Mistakenly, Karen had always thought Arnold had wanted the senior job.

'I'll see to it that the department is still here when you get back,' Arnold said, attempting a little levity. She was not amused.

'You ever heard of the FCAI?'

Arnold nodded. 'The Funding Council for Archaeological Investigation. A private charitable foundation, I understand, set up originally in Germany. But now . . .'

'The emphasis has become Europe-wide. It's the FCAI conference that I'm going to next week. I'll be presenting a paper. On the sea cave investigation up at Abbey Head.'

With which she had had relatively little to do. But that was the way of the professional world, and very much Karen's way, Arnold thought. 'You've got all the information you need?'

She nodded, almost dismissively. 'Of course. It will be my paper, based on the team's findings. The idea was that Portia would come along with me, help fill in any gaps in my own . . . understanding of the project.' She smiled. 'I know my limitations. I'm not a complete fool, Arnold.'

He had never thought she was, but he was surprised by the smile. 'I'm sure Portia will hardly be needed,' he suggested.

'Yes . . . I've come to that conclusion myself. The thing is, Arnold, I think it might be a better idea if you came along, instead.'

A silence grew between them. There was a sudden electricity in the air, a tension of which they were both aware. Arnold's mouth was dry. Karen's fingers crept up to the neck of her blouse, picked at it almost nervously. Then the words of explanation came out in a rush.

'The FCAI conference seems to me to be a perfect opportunity to try to solve some of our problems with Joe Holderness. I've spoken to him on the phone, and you're right. In spite of all the arguments I raised, he's not going to budge on time scales. So if we are to have any chance to complete our work at Fordbridge we've got to get more resources. Manpower means money. As I suspected, Powell Frinton won't release any funds. We've exhausted what's available to us from our Heritage contacts, but if we don't get some extra funding we're dead in the water. So I've decided to make an approach to the FCAI.'

'They've never previously funded a project in England, not to my knowledge,' Arnold managed to say, his thoughts still foolishly elsewhere as she uncrossed her legs and leaned forward.

Karen nodded. 'That's right. But one of the Board members of the foundation has recently taken up an appointment in the Department of African Studies at Newcastle University. A Dr Mwate. He's an expert on shamanic art. And his connections with the north-east go way back, it seems. Family. Anyway, I think an approach to him initially might help, in view of the artwork we found at the sea cave. And then there's James Stead, the FCAI chairman. I'm told he's . . . approachable.'

Her glance flickered up, held his challengingly. Arnold had heard of James Stead. An experienced archaeologist of international renown, sixty years of age, he was still noted for his philandering. And Karen Stannard was well used to using her femininity as well as her professional expertise to get what she wanted. The surge in his chest was dying. He suddenly felt very foolish. 'Where do I come into the equation? Surely, my time will be better spent keeping things running here—'

'No. It's time we gave Portia an opportunity to handle matters. And I think it's important you come to Carcassonne with me.'

Her eyes were suddenly evasive, a slight tinge of colour to her cheek. 'The fact is, you . . . you have a reputation. The *sudarium*, a few years back, Becket's seat the *Kvernbitr* . . . your name is known. And you were involved with the sea cave, even more so than Portia, so you could step in to handle any discussions about the shamanic drawings on the roof of the cave. Probably more effectively than she could.' Karen had not enjoyed making the complimentary remark. She ploughed on, hurriedly. 'I think you could have an influence on Mwate. Which you could follow up after the conference, when he's in Newcastle. Moreover, Dr Charles Midgley is vice-chairman of the funding subcommittee, and he's recently started research on chariot burials. You're the liaison officer for Fordbridge, so, all in all it seems to me, well . . . QED.'

Quod erat demonstrandum. She had given several reasons for his required presence at the Carcassonne conference, all of them ringing with conviction. And yet . . .

As though she sensed the unspoken questions in his mind she rose abruptly. 'You can get all the travel and accommodation details from my secretary. I take it there are no pressing private reasons why you wouldn't be able to make it?'

He shrugged, shook his head. He could think of none. She nodded and turned towards the door, but then she paused, looked back at him. There was a shadow of uncharacteristic anxiety in her eyes, a hesitancy that he had never seen in her before. It seemed she wanted to say something, but the words would not come. 'Arnold . . .'

He waited.

'We haven't really talked . . .'

The silence lengthened. She bit her lip and suddenly her control was back, dismissing signs of emotional weakness and indecision. He knew what was in her mind. If they hadn't talked previously about what had happened between them at Alnwick, this wasn't the time. Maybe it was an episode that was best left buried between them. She left him, closing the door quietly behind her.

Carcassonne. With Karen Stannard.

Arnold wondered what Jerry Picton would make of that.

2

The conference room at Ponteland HQ was completely silent as the recently appointed Assistant Chief Constable strode into the room. He was a big, heavily built man, well over six feet in height, immaculately suited, with iron-grey hair cut short, sharp blue eyes and a barracuda mouth. As he sat down in the leather-covered chair behind the desk at the far end of the room, O'Connor heard someone in the row behind him whisper, 'Used to play second row for Somerset Police, apparently, when they were a team to reckon with in West Country rugby. Eighteen stone of dynamite — but only an inch and a half of fuse.' There was a snigger. 'Had a short temper too, they reckon.'

The Assistant Chief Constable shuffled his bulk in the chair, looked up from the notes he had been perusing. His voice had an odd, grating quality. 'I won't waste time in pre-liminaries. For those who don't already know, my name is Sid Cathery. You'll all know I'm recently appointed. You've all been aware of the shake-up that's occurred in the force.' He paused, his eyes glittering as he glanced around the room. 'I've had long discussions with the new chief constable. Some of the practices which have been indulged in of recent years will no longer be permitted. I'm not going into details here and now. You'll know what I'm talking about. What I can tell you is that there's going to be more and tighter control from the centre. That's not just a fact. It's a warning.'

His eyes roved the room coldly. 'For this morning, I thought it would be a good idea to get you all together so that I can bring myself — and you — up to date with the operations that are currently proceeding. I have been told, by colleagues in the past, that when I'm pleased about something I have a tendency to rub my hands together. I'm not rubbing them at the moment, but maybe the senior officers in charge of operations will be able to change that situation.' He consulted his notes again. 'Let's begin with the Starlight Club business. DI Farnsby . . . I believe you've been handling the enquiry as far as our force is concerned.'

O'Connor glanced sideways at Farnsby, seated to his left. New to the force himself, he had had no opportunity to talk with the man at length since Detective Chief Inspector Culpeper had retired, but he knew that Farnsby would inevitably have been disappointed not to have succeeded Culpeper. Instead, they had drafted in O'Connor from Yorkshire. It had all been an inevitable consequence of the scandal that had broken about the head of the chief constable three months ago: quiet retirements to avoid public outcry had been necessary, and some in the force had suffered. O'Connor had heard that fast-track graduate Farnsby had been the blue-eyed boy of the previous Chief. All that was yesterday's news. The new brooms, inevitably, were sweeping clean and old loyalties would count for nothing. As DI Farnsby rose to his feet O'Connor stared at him with curiosity: dark-haired, lean, saturnine cast to his features, stony-eyed. Very much like O'Connor himself in looks, though maybe ten years younger.

'Operation Starlight has been all but concluded,' Farnsby was reporting. 'As we all know, it's been a long haul which has involved three separate police forces in the north, working to nail this group of men who've been trading in pay per view child pornography on the Internet. The websites in question have been charging customers a set rate which gave them access to a library of images for a limited period of time. I've been acting as liaison between the three forces concerned in the north-east, and the whole thing was co-ordinated from Durham. It all culminated in a series of dawn raids—'

'Did you take part in these personally?' ACC Cathery interrupted.

'No, sir. I—'

'So who did?'

'Our own teams were led by DS Robinson—'

'So let's hear from the horse's mouth.'

Thin-lipped, a little pale, Farnsby sat down. Thickset and red in the face, Detective Sergeant Robinson rose reluctantly. He was sweating visibly. 'We already had a considerable bank of information, sir, before we carried out the raids. Several of the men concerned were already known to us as child abusers. They were on the register. We've been working closely with other agencies naturally, and had built up a case for the CPS to consider but the raids were designed to pull in clinching evidence of the Internet use itself. We finally arrested nine men. A considerable amount of material and equipment was seized from the men's homes, and the men themselves have been taken to various police stations for questioning. They've come out with the usual sort of stuff—squealing that they don't think they've done anything wrong, they tell us we should be out looking for real criminals, what they been up to, it's all just innocent stuff, the kids concerned have really been asking for it . . . We've heard it all before.'

'But the group . . . the members of this so-called Starlight Club, they've all been hauled into the net?' Cathery queried.

Robinson hesitated, glanced uncertainly towards DI Farnsby. 'Well, we've done pretty well, but there's been a lot of stuff to go through . . .'

In the short silence that followed, Farnsby rose to his feet again, waited until Cathery nodded. The Assistant Chief Constable seemed to like that sort of recognition. 'What DS Robinson means is, we've not finished our interrogations yet, sir. The nine men we've arrested are still reluctant to talk, or incriminate each other, but we're getting there. Some of the names will be known to most of us in this room . . .' The Assistant Chief Constable waited patiently as Farnsby read out the list of names, to occasional murmurs from the men and women in the conference room. 'But we still have a few problems,' Farnsby continued.

'In particular?' Cathery queried.

'The individual who actually set up the website concerned, and established the Starlight Club. We don't have a name for him. We haven't been able to identify him.' Cathery frowned, there was no sign of him rubbing his hands. 'No identification at all? No one's talking?'

'They say they can't tell us. He's simply known among the group as The Doctor. None of the people we've arrested claim they're able to help. They deny knowing who he is. Just a name on the website. That's all.'

Assistant Chief Constable Cathery held Farnsby's glance for several seconds. He was clearly displeased. Farnsby showed no sign of flinching. O'Connor guessed that the man's resentment at his failure to get promotion still rankled, a deep iron in his soul. That resentment stiffened his sinews, facing the senior officer.

'All right,' Cathery muttered. 'We'll just have to await results. I hope they arrive soon. Let's move on.' He consulted the notes in front of him. 'DCI O'Connor . . . I believe you're handling the matter of this North Shields killing.'

O'Connor stood up and nodded. 'It's early days yet, sir.'

Cathery leaned back in his chair. 'So fill us in.'

O'Connor took a deep breath. 'We received an anonymous call from a telephone box in North Shields. It was brief, but sufficiently detailed to get us sending a squad car down to the Black Rocks at Shields. They radioed in immediately they saw what was there on the rocks. We had to act quickly before the tides changed in the river. A scene of crime unit was organized at once.'

'And they found?'

'A headless torso.'

'Man or woman?'

'A male child. Black.'

There was a long, pregnant silence in the room. 'I needn't emphasize the problems that we face here, sir,' O'Connor continued. 'We've had the initial report from the forensic labs, and it's not very helpful. I think we're going to have a big problem identifying this child, let alone finding out how the killing took place or who was responsible.'

'Let's get this clear,' Cathery growled, his brows coming together in concentration. 'Just a torso?'

'No head, arms or legs below the knee,' O'Connor confirmed.

'Clothing?'

O'Connor shook his head in regret. 'Just the remains of a pair of shorts. Tartan.' He paused. 'The torso was bundled up in heavy duty black polythene. The package had suffered some damage, the time it was in the river. There wasn't much left of the torso — flapping skin and ragged bones after the fish had picked at him. The legs had been severed just at the knee. The arms cut off at the shoulder.'

'Age?'

'Forensic suggest maybe seven or eight years old. Probably African, maybe four feet in height. He'd been in the water for several days. Post-mortem results show he died from a violent trauma to the neck, and that the limbs were removed after death.'

'To avoid identification,' Cathery rumbled gloomily.

'*Bastards*,' someone muttered behind O'Connor.

'We've put out a trawl,' O'Connor announced, 'but the problem is that no one seems to know anything about the child. No one has been reported missing in the area, no one to fit this description, for what it is. Nurseries and primary schools have been contacted; missing persons register; we've used all available computer bases, made public appeals, but not a single person has come forward.'

'No significant leads?'

'Nothing. There are no fingerprints to go on, of course. And no dental records. Obviously, the labs have been able to extract DNA material but at the moment it's of no help because we've nothing to make a match with it. No relatives we know of to provide hair fibres or anything else to give the forensic people a starting point.'

The Assistant Chief Constable grimaced. 'So we can all see the problem. No relevant missing person report, no limbs, no head . . . identification of a torso alone will be virtually impossible.'

O'Connor shrugged. 'Forensic say they can identify the victim's race, age, height, weight, approximately, and his general fitness and nutritional health. But that's about it. We're concentrating on the tartan shorts at the moment see if we can get any trace on them.'

'What about the anonymous caller?' Cathery asked. 'Still looking for him. We've got a trace on some kids who would also seem to have seen the plastic-wrapped torso. They came across it on the rocks, thought it was a beer keg at first. The smell made them call someone who was sitting on the promenade. He's probably the guy who phoned in.'

'But he hasn't come forward.'

O'Connor shook his head. 'He's keeping his head down. But we have a description.'

'Theories?'

'We have some, sir. Too early to elaborate,' O'Connor replied cautiously. 'But what we do need is more manpower.'

'Don't we always?' Cathery grunted. He stared at the sheets in front of him for a little while. Then he raised his iron-grey head and stared around the conference room. 'Okay . . . any questions . . . any point anyone wants to raise?'

For most of the officers in the room it didn't seem a good time. Assistant Chief Constable Cathery was an unknown entity to them: better to wait, and see how relationships panned out. The force had been too shaken by recent events for anyone to be prepared to make himself — or herself — too visible.

Assistant Chief Constable Cathery nodded. 'Right. That's it then. Just a few administrative matters now. And then . . . DI Farnsby . . . DCI O'Connor. My room please, immediately, this session is over.'

* * *

'Whenever you make a move for professional reasons, you come with baggage, isn't that right, O'Connor?'

Jack O'Connor sat up straight in his chair. He was not at ease. Cathery had called them to his room and then, surprisingly, offered them each a glass of whisky. O'Connor had accepted his, Farnsby had declined with a cool politeness. Cathery had not seemed offended. But he had made it clear that the whisky offer was to be a one-off event — a way of breaking some ice, introducing himself. Thereafter, formality would take over.

'I suppose that's inevitable, sir,' O'Connor replied carefully.

Cathery nodded. 'Up from York, I understand. But a Lancashire lad. Your father was a copper before you, but never made it beyond sergeant. Bog Irish, was he?'

Rank permitted certain privileges, O'Connor thought sourly. Like using insulting language. 'No, sir. He was Irish by descent, but three generations in Lancashire. Weavers, originally.' He could have gone on about senility and incontinence, crumbling memory in a crumbling face, Alzheimer-forgetful in a dark, dreary nursing home. He did not elaborate.

Cathery grunted and sipped at his whisky, leaned back in his chair. 'Mmm. And not your first time, working up here. Secondment last year? That was a bit messy too, wasn't it? Body fished out of the sea.'

He sipped again at his whisky, and raised a shaggy eyebrow. 'Marine animals your speciality then?'

O'Connor made no reply. Cathery grinned. 'So what baggage do you bring, O'Connor? I hear you didn't get on too well with your senior officers down at York. That make you apply to join us up here?'

'It seemed a good opportunity for promotion, to work in an environment I enjoyed,' O'Connor replied carefully.

'As long as you don't enjoy it too much,' Cathery warned. 'That's been the trouble up here for some time, in my view. Too much laxity, senior officers who'd forgotten how to handle reins. Everyone needs a strong, controlling hand.' His glance slipped to the man seated beside O'Connor, weighing him up. 'Which brings us to you, Farnsby.'

'Sir?'

'We all know that the chief constable had got a bit lazy, made too many friendships in the county set-up here, started doing favours, turning a blind eye to things he should have followed through on. That's on the record, now. And some of that . . . indulgence, it clearly rubbed off on his minions. It's why the former ACC went as well, when the Chief decided — on advice — to resign. Thing is, both men seemed to have a special soft spot for you. Now just what am I supposed to make of that?'

Stiff-backed, Farnsby replied, 'I just did my job to the best of my abilities.'

'But they liked the cut of your jib. Graduate, fast-tracked, showed promise. That's what the reports said. What about the man you worked with — DCI Culpeper?'

'We worked well enough together.'

The brief smile that touched Cathery's lips held a hint of malice. 'But didn't get on too well personally, I hear. Like O'Connor here, with his DCS. What is it with you men . . . too much independence of thought? You even look alike: Tweedledum and Tweedledee.' Cathery was silent for a little while, staring at the two men thoughtfully. 'However, like I said earlier, everyone comes with baggage. I'm no exception. I've been around a while, and, well, there's people I've been in contact with, you know what I mean? And when a name leaps out of a report . . .' His eyes glinted thoughtfully. 'I've been trawling through the backlog of files, sort of getting acquainted with what's been going on up here. And there's one enquiry that seems to have been . . . shall we say . . .

wound down to some extent. Would that have been the chief constable's doing?'

Farnsby's voice was strained. 'Which enquiry are you referring to, sir?'

Cathery smiled grimly. 'Nothing that rated great priority, it seems. Expensive cars, being shipped out of the country. I've seen the files. They've been top line stuff Mercedes, Porsches, BMWs. Quite a few nicked from Darras Hall, I gather, posh areas of Durham, all organized, probably stolen to order. Suspected to have been shipped to Rotterdam by way of the Hull ferry. But after initial investigations, everything seems to have been . . . slowed. Why is that, you know?'

Farnsby glanced at O'Connor and shrugged diffidently. 'Not for me to say, sir. I wasn't involved with the case. I gather the enquiry wasn't going anywhere, the pressure was taken off and the thefts themselves dwindled. The decision was taken at the top level.'

Cathery nodded, his eyes gleaming. 'So it seems. Well, the news is that it's going to be reopened. As of now. I don't think we need go into reasons why it was wound down as an enquiry — the people concerned have gone, anyway. But it's time we hauled in the guys who were behind this business. I want it made a priority.'

O'Connor raised his head. 'Is this some of the baggage *you're* bringing, sir?'

Cathery sat very still, his cold eyes fixed on O'Connor. For a few moments he seemed to be about to explode, but then his shoulders relaxed. 'You could say that,' he replied softly. 'I've been reading the reports. A raid on a garage in South Shields. A man was questioned, but not held. Name of Catford.' He smiled thinly. 'We're old acquaintances, Don Catford and I. I think I'd be pleased if we were to . . . renew the acquaintance. In the right kind of circumstances.' He paused, grimly. 'No one likes being made to look foolish, do they? I have a score to settle with Don Catford.' His glance slipped away from O'Connor, to fix on Farnsby. 'You'll be taking over the files.'

Farnsby leaned forward, a frown gathering on his face. 'Stolen cars, sir?'

'Correct.'

'But the Starlight enquiry . . . I've got my hands full—'

'You've already said the perpetrators are in custody. Except for this man they call The Doctor. He'll be landed soon enough, I don't doubt. Someone will talk. It's basic legwork from now on. The case has been cracked. So, Detective Sergeant Robinson can take over from now on. He'll act as liaison.'

Farnsby flushed. 'Sir, I don't think—'

'But I do!' Cathery took a slow sip of his whisky, waved the glass negligently in Farnsby's direction. 'Look at it from my point of view. I want this South Shields enquiry proceeded with, and with more urgency. No more back-handers, no more looking after friends in high places. A priority, me being the new broom around here. Now DCI O'Connor, he's a new broom too and I want him to have the chance to prove himself. He'll be handling the torso business. Headhunter, yes?' Cathery snickered to himself. 'Operation Headhunter.'

Farnsby bridled. 'But the Starlight enquiry—'

'Will be handled by Robinson,' Cathery insisted, an edge of steel entering his tone. 'You don't seem to get the picture, Farnsby. O'Connor here, I'm at ease with him. Maybe because I don't know him, and he's an outsider, like me. He's got a furrow to plough and the field is clean ahead of him. But you . . . you were the former Chief's blue-eyed boy. Now he may have been right in his judgements. On the other hand, we now know there were many judgements he made which . . . well, they ended up with him taking early retirement, you know what I mean? So I don't have much to go on as far as you're concerned. It follows that I see this as a kind of proving ground for you, Farnsby. Show me what you're made of. I want you to think of yourself as a pistol muzzle, pointing straight at a man called Don Catford. His name came up in the earlier Shields enquiry. The mere fact his name is there, that's enough for me. I want him nailed to a fencepost. Show me you're the man who can do it.'

Farnsby was controlling himself with difficulty. 'Personal vendettas can cloud judgement, sir.'

Cathery smiled coldly. 'But it's *my* personal vendetta, son. Not yours. And you're the one who'll be reopening the enquiry. With a target in mind. Clear?'

Farnsby sat back in his chair, his face blank. O'Connor had a certain sympathy for him. He drained his whisky glass, replaced it on the desk in front of him. Cathery raised a quizzical eyebrow. 'So, are we all in the picture now?'

Both men facing him nodded without speaking. Cathery gave them a cold smile. 'Good. Well, I expect results sooner rather than later.' He raised a hand, flicked his fingers dismissively. 'I'm pleased we've been able to have this little chat. Get a few things straight.'

When the door closed behind them and they walked along the corridor the two officers were silent. The taste of Cathery's whisky was sour in O'Connor's mouth. He glanced at Farnsby. 'I could do with a real drink.'

The detective inspector stopped at the glass doors leading to the stairs. 'Not for me, thanks.'

O'Connor put his hand on the younger man's shoulder. 'Look, Farnsby, I—'

He saw the coldness in the man's eyes and removed his hand. He frowned. 'I . . . I just wanted to say I appreciate the way you feel. Culpeper's retirement—'

'You can't possibly know or appreciate how I feel,' Farnsby hissed. 'I'm being victimized here. I had every expectation of succeeding Culpeper, becoming DCI. I make no secret of my ambition, Culpeper hung on too long, and I worked hard to get that job. It wasn't my fault that the Old Man went off the rails, and dragged other senior officers with him. I got on with my job, worked with that old bastard Culpeper, and I got results. And now this arrogant sod Cathery waltzes in here, comes in with his talk of new brooms and proving myself . . . I've *already* proved myself! More than a few times! And what do I get for it? I get shoved off on to a half-arsed enquiry that folded for lack of evidence months ago!'

O'Connor's sympathy was waning. 'Look, it's no good taking it out on me. We have to work together, and—'

'No,' Farnsby flashed angrily. 'You and I, we don't have to work together. We're on different enquiries. We don't even have to like each other. I didn't like Culpeper. And you're the one who got Culpeper's job.' He turned away, thrust through the glass doors to the stairs. 'You got the job and you can bloody well get on with it!'

3

Their flights from Newcastle to Stansted and on thereafter to
Carcassonne were uneventful. A conference car was waiting
for Arnold and Karen at the airport to take them to their hotel
in the medieval city. Shortly after, they arrived and booked
into the hotel in the heart of the city, Karen Stannard rang
through to Arnold's room. She announced that she would be
having dinner with James Stead, before the conference itself
got under way the following day. Arnold had no doubt she
would be using her feminine charms to begin the offensive,
and realized it was good tactics to allow her to impress herself
upon the susceptible chairman of the FCAI without Arnold
in tow. Arnold had no problem with the strategy. It gave
him the opportunity to leave the hotel and walk around the
walled town by himself.

The conference members were all staying at the same
hotel in the centre of La Cité, overlooking the lower, more
modern town, the Ville Basse. Arnold was aware that the
residents of La Cité were few, of course. The ancient town,
dating back to the fourth century, was now almost entirely
given over to the pursuit of tourism. But this meant that
Arnold was able to wander into the square and find a restaurant in Place du Château, enjoy the mild evening air, watch

the passing throng and order a traditional cassoulet of pork, haricot beans, mutton and preserved goose, cooked, the waiter assured him, in an earthenware pot in the time-honoured manner, over a fire of gorse twigs gathered from the Montagne Noire.

He did not see Karen that evening when he returned to the hotel. She had probably escaped James Stead after dinner by pleading tiredness, for Arnold caught sight of the FCAI chairman in the hotel bar, bald head gleaming, waving a gin and tonic and discoursing to some of his hangers-on, most of whom, Arnold noted, appeared to be relatively young and female. Stead was clearly gender conscious: he preferred the company of young women.

Some of the delegates were still due to arrive the following morning since the conference did not commence its opening session until a formal lunch, so Arnold rose early, forgoing the hotel breakfast, and found a small cafe in Place Marcou where he could fortify himself with good strong coffee and croissants before undertaking a tour of the ancient walls of the medieval city.

The Visigoths had captured Carcassonne in the fifth century. It had fallen to the Franks three hundred years later; and its prosperity had been interrupted only in the thirteenth century by the carnage of the Albigensian Crusade, when the citizens of Carcassonne had refused to give up the Cathars they protected. Much of the walled city had later been repaired and reinforced by Philip the Bold but restoration had been decided upon in 1844 and the results were impressive. Arnold walked the ramparts of the Cité, seeking signs of the restoration, and noting the evidence of the earlier constructions: the crenelated redoubt of the Porte Narbonnaise with its arrow-slitted barbican, the twelfth-century Château Comtal, the Tour de Justice where the protectors of the Cathars had sought refuge during the Albigensian Crusade from the army of Simon de Montfort.

There was a scattering of tourists and guided groups in the Cité and as he walked the walls and made his way through the winding medieval streets Arnold became aware of one particular small group seemingly intent on undertaking the same kind of walking tour as he had decided upon. The two women were young, probably in their early twenties, but their companion was older, perhaps forty years of age, a huge black man, well over six feet in height, dark-suited, with massive shoulders and a chest that seemed to strain at his jacket. He had a presence that could be described only as formidable. His thick hair was short, tightly curled; his broad face was animated, alive with laughter, smiling as he teased the women. His red-rimmed eyes were alight with mischief. He had a booming laugh which rang out uninhibitedly, echoing around the Cour de Midi, bouncing back off the walls of the well-preserved watchtower. It was only when Arnold stood near them in the Tour de l'Inquisition that the big man seemed to become a little more reserved. He was standing just in front of Arnold in the tower, and he turned his head enquiringly, gestured towards the central pillar with its chains. 'Torture?' he suggested to Arnold.

'That's right. This place was the seat of the court of the Inquisition,' Arnold replied. 'The Cathar heretics were tortured here, and imprisoned in the cell below.'

The big man grunted. 'Nothing much changes. But in my own country, right now, the heresy is to disagree not with the established church, but with the government. Or be white. That's enough in itself.' He managed a slow smile, edged with cynicism. 'Zimbabwe.'

Arnold nodded, and moved on.

He spent some time in the lapidary looking at the exhibits of archaeological remains from the fortified town itself and the local region before exiting again into the narrow winding streets of the medieval town, past the inevitable cluster of craft and souvenir shops catering to the tourist trade, selling books and postcards and photographs, paintings and general clutter. He moved on, inspecting the inner western ramparts, and the Basilique St-Nazaire, before he found a cafe where he could take a break, ordering another grand cafe and a cognac. While he sat there, he caught sight of the big Zimbabwean again, walking along the Rue Cros-Mayrevieille, advising the two young women as they picked over souvenirs, laughing, joking, all three clearly enjoying the morning in the Cité. And after Arnold had finished his coffee, when he was walking through the Porte d' Aude to enjoy the view over the river towards the Ville Basse, he came across them again on the fortified path of the Monté d'Aude. The big Zimbabwean recognized him, raised a hand, came forward, smiling broadly.

'Ah, my knowledgeable friend of the Tour de l'Inqui-sition. You might be able to help us. The girls have been puzzled, and they won't take my word, since I am not an expert in the French language.' He gestured towards a sign on the wall above him. 'This name — *lices basses* — I have told them it refers to small animals that cause you to scratch in your lower regions. You are able to confirm this?'

Arnold grinned, shook his head. 'No, I'm afraid not. It's the name given to sections of the outer bailey of La Cité, and the oldest stretch of the inner curtain wall, built by the Visigoths.'

'Indeed,' the Zimbabwean replied, eyeing Arnold spec-ulatively. 'So I am also wrong about the *lices hautes*.'

'He said it meant head lice,' one of the giggling girls intervened.

Arnold smiled at the grinning Zimbabwean and shook his head regretfully. 'I think maybe your friend has been reading the wrong books. The term refers to the outer bailey east of the fortified Cité, where the gap between the inner and outer ramparts is very wide. They used the area for weap-ons practice and jousting.'

The big Zimbabwean shrugged his massive shoulders in mock resignation and raised expressive hands. 'You see, girls, you have made a big mistake. You should have paid for a guide, rather than rely on me.' He lifted one eyebrow, smiled at Arnold, his eyes seeming to weigh him up, measure him. 'My guess is you know a great deal, and will also be able to date much of this fortified city. Up there, for instance, the small bond walls with brickwork levelling out the masonry courses . . .'

'Gallo-Roman era. Third century,' Arnold replied soberly.

'On the defensive walls they used rectangular grey stones—'

'Thirteenth century,' Arnold said abruptly, playing along.

The man's eyes widened in mock respect. 'And the rustic masonry and the projections on the towers, shaped like the beaks of our own Zimbabwean bird-symbol?'

'The reign of Philip the Bold.'

The big black man assumed a fierce frown. 'Are you sure you aren't employed by the tourist board? I was out to impress these young ladies, but you have taken the wind from my sails. How is it you know so much about La Cité? You must be a great expert.'

Arnold shook his head. 'No . . . I just read the Michelin Green Guide last night.'

He moved away as the Zimbabwean exploded with laughter.

* * *

A formal lunch was available for conference members in the hotel but Arnold decided to give it a miss and take further advantage of the local cuisine in the town. He sat in the square under the gaily coloured protective awnings, shaded from the hot sun, enjoying the chatter and buzzing excitement of the square. At two o'clock he decided he had better return to the hotel: the official opening of the conference was slated for three o'clock. He went back to his room, took a shower and changed into a dark suit. He met Karen on the stairs as he was going down to the conference room.

She eyed him in mock appreciation. 'That's more like it. I saw you going out earlier. You were dressed like a tourist.'

'I *was* a tourist this morning.'

'We're not paying for you to have a holiday.'

'From now on, it's all business,' he assured her. 'Talking of holidays, how did you get on with James Stead last night?'

She grimaced. 'Hardly a time for relaxation. I needed to have my wits about me, and my guard up. I didn't manage to get too much business done. He had his mind on other things.'

'I can imagine,' Arnold smiled. 'But I've no doubt you managed to retain your honour. I saw him in the bar late last night, with an entourage.'

'Mainly female, no doubt. A migraine always helps, as a plea to escape. But I did manage to get some basic information across to him during dinner, about the Fordbridge site and its importance. I think it got through. My guess is he'll support us. Just how influential he is with the committee, of course, we've yet to discover.' She eyed him appraisingly. 'And did you enjoy yourself last night in the fleshpots of Carcassonne?'

'The illuminated city looked wonderful.'

'You'll have to show me.'

She walked into the conference hall ahead of him. Arnold was a little taken aback at her last comment. She rarely relaxed enough in his company to indulge in light banter, or issue an invitation. Perhaps the location, the medieval French atmosphere, had made an impact. Certainly there was no sign of the tension that had existed between them in the office, when they had discussed coming to Carcassonne. He felt confused. As he had been confused ever since that night in Alnwick. He glanced at her profile as he took a seat beside her in the main body of the conference room. She seemed as cool and confident as ever, but he realized she was aware of his scrutiny and there was a hint of satisfaction about her mouth. Then he was distracted as the platform party took their seats.

James Stead led the group but Arnold was surprised at its make-up. Third to arrive on the platform was the big, laughing Zimbabwean he had met earlier that morning at the ramparts.

As chairman of the FCAI James Stead opened the conference with a welcoming speech. He introduced the platform party: the first speaker, Professor Woodward; members of the committee — Dr Martin Woudt from the Rijksmuseum in Amsterdam, Dr Charles Midgley, forensic scientist from the Northern Laboratories and Dr Pierre Forray, from the Sorbonne. The big Zimbabwean was introduced as Dr Julian Mwate. Arnold was startled to hear that he was employed at the University of Newcastle.

Professor Woodward, slight, bespectacled, was not a great speaker, and although Arnold found his topic interesting — *The Architectural Impact of Roman, Celtic and Christian Shrines upon Local Environments* — the droning presentation itself was too long, and the man's flat, monotonous tones caused a number of people in the audience to lose interest early on. Glancing around at the audience, Arnold caught sight of the two young women Dr Mwate had been escorting around the Cité that morning. Both had dozed off. Clearly, shrines were not their scene.

At the conclusion of Woodward's lecture the conference broke for tea, and returned for a second session before dinner, Dr Pierre Forray speaking on *The Central Role Played by Groves and Natural Features in Pagan Celtic Ideologies*. Arnold — and the rest of the audience — found it easier to cope with than Woodward's presentation, and Forray spoke excellent English. When the lecture was concluded and the answer session was over, Karen leaned towards Arnold. 'Dinner's at eight, but things are moving faster than I'd anticipated. James Stead spoke to me at the tea break. We won't be eating with the conference members tonight. A dining room has been reserved for us to dine privately.'

'You mean you and Stead?' Arnold asked mischievously.

She dug him in the ribs. 'This is serious. Not a *tête-à-tête* — though I suspect he might want to follow up later. No, it's just you, me and the funding committee. They want to talk with us over dinner, away from the main conference. Looks like James Stead wants to move things on.'

Arnold could guess why. Knowing the man's predilections, he would want to get an early favourable decision from the committee, so that he could bask — before the conference ended — in the grateful warmth of Karen Stannard's smile. What Stead didn't know, Arnold thought to himself, was that Karen Stannard was not so easily seduced. There had been more than a few who had tried, and with far more sophisticated techniques. To no effect.

They met for cocktails before dinner. Stead himself — portly and bald, but with youthful eyes and a confident smile — quickly attached himself to Karen, who was dazzling in a white sheath dress that emphasized her tanned skin and clung to the outlines of her figure. Stead managed to manoeuvre her away from the main body of the group, but was clearly irritated by the way in which the Frenchman, Forray, remained in tow, suitably encouraged by Karen as part of her defensive strategy. Arnold found himself standing with Martin Woudt as Charles Midgley came to join them.

'Ah, so you two already know each other,' Midgley said, waving his glass.

'Well, not really,' Arnold confessed. He glanced at the slimly built, hawkish-featured, middle-aged man standing beside him. 'We've just got as far as naming names.'

'Of course, Martin I know — we're fellow members of the committee. So as the only male stranger in the room, you must be Arnold Landon,' Midgley remarked, baring his teeth in a smile that seemed more predatory than welcoming.

'That's right.'

'We've all heard of your work,' Martin Woudt commented diffidently.

'I'm surprised.'

'You should not be,' Woudt said in a cool tone. He flicked a piece of fluff from his immaculately cut jacket, and adjusted the handkerchief that was neatly folded in his breast pocket. He had a long, rather lugubrious face with sad, intense eyes, and his mouth seemed marked with a strange doubt, as if of self-criticism, uncertainty about his own worth. 'Your history in northern archaeological circles has been well remarked upon. You have been remarkably successful in unearthing important artefacts—'

'Luck,' Arnold suggested deprecatingly.

'An important quality for an archaeologist,' Woudt insisted. 'It's in the eyes, is it not, and the hands? No matter how many academic qualifications one possesses, in the end if one cannot see and feel . . .' He looked at his own hands. His fingers were long, slender, carefully manicured.

'But I could never aspire to the kind of work you've done in the Rijksmuseum,' Arnold countered.

'Ha! A mere curator. It's not the same thing,' Woudt replied dismissively. 'No, it is well known that while you are what many would describe as an amateur archaeologist, you nevertheless have achieved remarkable results. But then, such a description is attached to my friend Dr Midgley here. Charles,' he said, touching the man affectionately on the shoulder, 'is really a forensic scientist.'

'Who treats archaeology as a hobby,' Midgley agreed. 'But, I suppose, the two disciplines are so closely related these days. And they raise similar issues: the amount of interpretation, and guesswork that becomes necessary. But there is a difference. From archaeology, no pressure. From the police . . . well, there is only so much one can obtain in a forensic examination, and the police rarely seem to be satisfied with what one offers. They want an interpretation that fits the theories they've been developing, and it can cause a great deal of friction when one is unable to go along with them and produce impressionistic views that are not strictly in accordance with the hard evidence derived from the forensics.'

'I suppose,' Woudt commented casually, 'they'll have theories about your latest little problem.'

Charles Midgley had a square-set face, and a belligerent, combative mouth. Like James Stead he was bald, but the baldness of his skull was somehow accentuated by the beetling thickness of his eyebrows. He drew them together now, squinting suspiciously at his colleague. 'What problem are you talking about?'

Woudt laughed, a little nervously. His eyes were evasive, flickering glances around the room. 'I am embarrassed. Sorry, Charles, I know you don't like discussing cases you have in hand. But I imagine in view of the recent discovery in your area, and the publicity it has generated, it's unlikely you would not be involved in the work.'

Midgley grimaced, looked at Arnold and shrugged. 'I suppose there's no harm in talking about it, because I don't believe we're ever going to get much from the forensics. After all, what do we have to work on?'

'What is the case?' Arnold asked curiously.

Midgley grunted, ran a hand over his bald head. 'You must have read about it in the newspapers. Front page news for a time. Headless body discovered in the Tyne, off North Shields. Just a torso: head and limbs removed. Clumsily perhaps, but effectively.'

'But you talked of police theories earlier. What lines are they following on this one?' Woudt asked diffidently, glancing around the room as though he were merely making conversation, and not terribly interested in the answer.

Midgley sipped at his drink, and pulled a face. 'To tell you the truth, they're not putting much pressure on. They're pretty much at a loss, don't know where to start. So they're *asking* me, for a change, rather than telling me what they want to hear. Ha, Julian,' he said, turning to meet the man joining them. 'You arrive at an opportune moment. We're talking about something that may well involve you very shortly.'

It was the big, cheerful Zimbabwean. He nodded to Woudt, smiled at Midgley and then extended his hand to Arnold. 'We met this morning,' he said in a deep, rich voice, 'but didn't really introduce ourselves. You're Arnold Landon. Had I known who you were at the time, our conversation would have been quite different.'

'But perhaps less entertaining for your companions.'

'I saw you walking out of the hotel with those two women,' Midgley said accusingly, jabbing Mwate with a stubby forefinger.

'Research students,' Julian Mwate explained cheerfully. 'I was taking them on an exploratory tour of La Cité.'

'Rubbish,' Midgley expostulated. 'I've seen the way you operate. In fact, every time I see you, it seems you have at least two women on your arm. How do you manage it, anyway?'

'Black magic,' Julian Mwate replied, and winked at Arnold. 'However, what was this comment you made when I joined you, Charles? What have you let me in for now?'

Midgley finished his glass, and deftly deposited it, taking another from the tray borne by a passing waiter. 'The murder case in Newcastle. You know, the headless torso.'

The ever-present smile on Julian Mwate's broad face seemed to harden slightly at the edges. 'The decapitated black boy,' he murmured.

'No head, no limbs, that's it,' Midgley replied waving his glass. 'I've given your name to the police.'

There was a short silence. Martin Woudt's head swivelled, his eyes fixed intensely on Charles Midgley. Julian Mwate shifted his bulk from one foot to another. He affected a downcast, guilty expression. 'I hopes you hasn't told them it was me wot done it, guv.'

Midgley burst out laughing, and punched Mwate playfully on his heavy upper arm. 'Better make sure you have an alibi, my friend. No, of course not. I gave them your name, because they're all at sea. They don't seem to know which way to turn. They've got a new man in charge, and the case has landed on his desk: a DCI called O'Connor, just drafted in recently from York, I understand. I've had a chat with him.'

'So why give him my name?' Mwate asked softly. 'What makes you think I can help the police in this matter?'

'Well, you know. What we talked about once. *Muti*. The practice of traditional medicine in Africa . . .' He was about to continue when he looked across the room, saw James Stead raising his hand. 'Ha! That's our revered chairman making a move.' He drained his glass swiftly. 'Come on, lads. Time to go in for dinner. Shall I lead on, gentlemen ?'

James Stead had, predictably, seated himself next to Karen. Arnold found himself opposite Professor Forray and between Dr Mwate and Professor Woodward. The professor on his left turned out to be as diffident as his lecture had been uninspired, and had little to say for himself. Mwate, on the other hand, was ebullient, witty and garrulous. He chatted easily, enquiring after Arnold's own experiences in the field, talking about the political situation in Zimbabwe, retailing amusing anecdotes from his time spent in the Andes and central America. Arnold enjoyed his company, particularly since the meal turned out to be a special one laid on for the group.

Cassoulet, prepared in the traditional fashion.

'You don't look too impressed,' Mwate suggested, gesturing at Arnold's untouched plate and widening his eyes in surprise.

'One can have too much of a good thing,' Arnold admitted. He suspected the so-called 'traditional' dish had in fact emerged from a tin. 'So you teach at Newcastle University.'

'That's right. I've taught in Harare and London previously, but now the university at Newcastle has been so unwise as to grant me a chair in the new Department of African Studies. I suspect it's not because of my qualifications, more likely because I'm a Geordie.'

'You're from Newcastle?' Arnold asked, unable to keep the surprise out of his voice.

'Isn't it obvious, man?' Mwate replied, flattening his vowels, grinning widely, his eyes alight with mischief. 'No, it's true enough. The fact is I was born in Fenham but the family went back to Zimbabwe in 1975. Of course, the country of my fathers holds little for me now — so you can say I've got back to my real roots. If you can accept a black Geordie.'

'What's your own speciality?' Arnold asked.

Mwate was trying the cassoulet, and his eyes widened in appreciation. 'Hey, if you really don't want yours, you'll have to pass it over! This is just like home cooking! And I'm a big lad.' He took a huge spoonful and rolled his eyes. 'Right . . . now then, my speciality? Well, I've done a certain amount of research on shamanic influences, so to some extent you played a part in my achieving the chair.'

'How do you make that out?' Arnold asked, puzzled. 'I'd read the reports on the shamanic influences present in the sea cave at Abbey Head. Interesting stuff. I look forward to hearing Miss Stannard talk about it to the conference tomorrow. The university appointments committee was somewhat impressed that I knew about the sea cave and agreed I could work on that among other things. Assuming your department would be interested in collaboration, of course. I haven't made the approach yet.'

'You'd need to talk to Karen Stannard about that,' Arnold suggested, 'but I can't see her turning the offer of assistance down. We're pretty short of funds and manpower, let alone expertise, and in view of some of the artefacts we've found at the recent dig at Fordbridge—'

'Ah, yes, James Stead was talking to us about that this morning. Before I . . . ah . . . sneaked off with the girls.' Mwate nodded thoughtfully and took a deep, satisfied breath. 'This cassoulet is good . . . and if what Stead tells the committee about the Fordbridge burial is correct, that should be a pretty good thing too.' He prodded his spoon into the juices of the cassoulet, searching out the meat. 'Indeed, if we can find shamanic links between the chariot burial and the sea cave, that could be an interesting prospect, don't you think?'

Arnold toyed with his own meal, took a sip of his red wine. 'Is what Dr Midgley mentioned . . . *muti*, was it — is that also tied in with African shamanic practices?' Arnold asked.

He was suddenly aware that some of Mwate's easy-going manner deserted him. He was silent for a few moments, pondering as he stared at a piece of pork on his spoon. He shrugged. 'My studies of shamanic practices have, necessarily, been largely concerned with parts of the world other than Africa. I've looked at Australia, New Guinea, Germany; much is to be seen in Celtic and Norse mythology, and even ancient Greek cultures contain striking shamanistic elements. Then there's Russia, the Central Asian steppes, India and the Americas — there's so much to investigate, don't you agree? A lifetime's work, really. But Africa, it's different.'

'How do you mean?'

'In most African cultures, people don't travel to the world of the spirits — the spirits come to this world. Trance occurs when people are possessed rather than when they call the spirits and control them, as is generally the case elsewhere.' He paused, reflectively. 'I suppose the Bushmen of the Kalahari break the mould. They claim to be able to climb to the sky — as would appear to be the case in the ancient culture shown in your cave drawings at Abbey Head.'

'But this *muti* — doesn't it have a basis in medicine, as the shamans practise it elsewhere in the world?'

'*Muti* is not quite the same thing,' Mwate replied shortly.

'How do you mean?'

Arnold was receiving the distinct impression that Dr Julian Mwate was reluctant to discuss the matter. The big man sighed, looked around the room at the others enjoying their meal. 'You have to understand, Mr Landon, right across Southern Africa there is an historical reliance on traditional, rather than modern medicine. This is what is called *muti*.' He hesitated. 'The word is derived from *umu thi*.'

'Which means?'

'It just means tree, really, but anyway the word has become a byword for traditional medicine, whether it's good or bad.'

'A sort of herbal folklore,' Arnold suggested.

Mwate shrugged. 'You could say that.' His broad, cheerful face had taken on a more sombre aspect. 'And it is practised not by shamans, as healing is practised by the Chukchi in Siberia, the Iban in Borneo, and shamans elsewhere in the world. No, in Africa it's practised by the *sangomas*. And the apparently benign intent of their medicine can sometimes mask a much darker, more sinister purpose. But enough of such matters . . .' He managed a smile. 'So tell me, what's it like working with such a beautiful creature as Karen Stannard?'

As he struggled to answer without disclosing the kinds of tensions which had long existed between himself and his head of department, Arnold realized he was being skilfully side-tracked. He was left wondering just why the forensic scientist Dr Midgley would have recommended Julian Mwate to the police, and what part the practice of *muti* might play in the police investigation of the headless torso discovered in the Tyne.

CHAPTER TWO

1

The following morning Karen Stannard made her planned conference presentation on the sea cave at Abbey Head. It was clear that the audience found the whole thing riveting. They had obviously read a great deal about the investigation, not simply because of the importance of the finds in the cave below the vulvic opening on the cliff top known for centuries as Hades Gate. There had also been the considerable publicity generated by the violence, and resonance of the past, that had been associated with the dig.

But Karen's presentation itself was also stimulating. She was dressed in a formal dark-blue suit with a white blouse which, while emphasizing her professionalism, did nothing to detract from her beauty. Her voice was clear and well modulated. She made the important points with the right degree of emphasis, her slide illustrations were models of clarity and appositeness, and the audience was gripped by her account. It had been her earlier intention to bring Portia Tyrrel with her, to answer any points she could not, but she had brought Arnold instead, in the event, his assistance was not required. As questions poured thick and fast from the audience she answered with ease, and there was no necessity for recourse to him. She had briefed herself properly and professionally.

She had mastered the information obtained from the Abbey Head site. She held the audience in the palm of her hand. Arnold admired her. Whatever difficulties she raised in the office, she was in his opinion a consummate professional.

The audience knew it too.

James Stead had chaired the session. His rubicund face was glowing with pleasure when he brought the question session to an end. He was acting as though she was his own personal protégé as he thanked her for the presentation. There was also a hint of relief in his eyes. After the presentation by Professor Woodward the previous day, something was needed to lift the occasion, and bring credibility to the organization of the conference. As they left the conference hall, Dr Mwate touched Arnold on the arm. 'I think I'm going to enjoy working with Miss Stannard, if it can be arranged.'

Arnold looked at his beaming features and smiled. 'If you do come on board with the further investigation of the sea cave, it's not Karen you'll be working with. But I can tell you, you'll also enjoy working with her assistant.'

Dr Julian Mwate had yet to meet Portia Tyrrel. She would certainly make him forget his research students.

After the coffee break the conference delegates split into interest groups, with discussion topics already designated. Arnold had been allocated to a group discussing maritime archaeology, which he knew little about but would be keen to explore, but in the event he had barely settled in with the group before one of the secretarial staff entered the room and sought him out. 'Would you mind following me, Mr Landon?' she whispered earnestly. 'Mr Stead has called a meeting of the FCAI committee and you and Miss Stannard are required to be present.'

Arnold made his apologies to the woman chairing, and left the group, following the young secretary down the corridor to the room which had served as a private dining room the previous evening. The others were already there: James Stead, seated at the head of a large circular table; Professor Forray in a floral tie and white suit, Dr Mwate, smiling a welcome at Arnold, Dr Midgley, looking a little the worse for wear after his post-dinner drinking, Dr Woudt staring at the table, face expressionless, and two other members of the committee who had not been able to be present for the opening sessions of the conference because of their university commitments. They were introduced as Professors Carter and Hunter as Arnold took the empty chair beside Karen. He noted that she had the Fordbridge folder on the table in front of her.

'I thought we should have this meeting earlier rather than later,' James Stead explained, 'so that we can then relax and enjoy the conference papers without other things on our minds. I have already had the privilege of a long discussion with Miss Stannard regarding her recent project — the chariot, or wagon burial at Fordbridge. I must say that I find it a most interesting opportunity for us to consider. And she has been most eloquent in pursuing the possibility of our being financially involved in the dig. As you know, gentlemen, we have rarely ventured across the Channel with our projects . . . but perhaps politically the time is ripe. Perhaps you would like to highlight the possibilities inherent in the Fordbridge investigation, Miss Stannard, for the benefit of our members.'

On arriving at the conference each delegate had been presented with a slim black leather document case emblazoned with a gilt FCAI logo. Karen reached down now to her feet and retrieved hers, opened it, extracted a sheaf of papers and passed them to Arnold for distribution.

As he walked around the table handing out the papers she began. 'While I have the full report here in front of me, I've made a summary among the papers you're receiving of the current state of the excavation at Fordbridge,' she explained. 'I thought it best to supply you with this information which highlights the importance of the dig. I will simply talk about the problems my department currently faces in furthering the work there, not least because of the pressure being put upon us by the site owner, Mr Holderness—'

'That's the property developer,' Stead intervened by way of explanation. 'He's given the project a deadline.'

Karen inclined her head gracefully, bestowing a smile on the chairman, and Stead beamed. Arnold was amused. Karen Stannard certainly knew how to handle the ageing roué. 'The site itself,' Karen continued, 'is not a spectacular one. A scatter of pits and postholes, a few small ring ditches . . . but at an early stage we were struck by the isolated, figure-of-eight-shaped pit . . .'

Arnold listened as she led the committee through the process of the investigation, emphasizing they were dealing with the last remains of a unique Iron Age chariot burial. Wheel remains had already been lifted intact in blocks of soil to be excavated in the laboratory. Initial indications showed traces of mineralized wood.

'Has anything survived of the corpse itself?' Midgley enquired, ever the forensic scientist.

'A few scraps of tooth enamel and the skeleton itself of course, with an iron mirror over the feet. The main thing is that such a find is rare in Britain. Perhaps, Chairman, you would allow Mr Landon to explain?'

Karen Stannard was mellowing, Arnold considered. There had been a time when she would never have handed over the floor to him. She would have kept the limelight on herself. On the other hand, perhaps it was because she was already confident of the outcome of the meeting, after her private discussions with James Stead.

In view of the nature of his audience and the European bias of the FCAI Arnold took the opportunity to stress the close parallels between the Fordbridge chariot burial and the well-documented Continental burials in Champagne and the Belgian Ardennes. He theorized about possible links with Europe, suggesting the woman interred might have been an immigrant or someone trading across the Channel and saw approval in the eyes of members of the committee. He commented on Continental burial rites and saw Martin Woudt betray greater interest. When he spoke of the inlaid glass enamels that closely resembled those that had been found on the Battersea Shield, Stead himself leaned forward, chin in hand, listening carefully to Arnold's presentation. Arnold made sure he also mentioned links with shamanic burial practices, and reflected upon certain similarities in the grave artefacts and the drawings on the walls and roof of the sea cave at Abbey Head.

'An investigation which is still proceeding,' he heard Julian Mwate murmur in satisfaction.

When Arnold had completed his presentation he leaned back. He caught Karen's glance, she nodded approvingly. James Stead looked around him importantly. 'Well, I think that helps us along to a considerable extent. Miss Stannard, Mr Landon, we're very grateful for the professional manner in which you've conducted this presentation. I feel sure the committee won't be too long in reaching a decision, but you'll appreciate that we will need to have a private discussion. So if you wouldn't mind leaving us now, for a while . . . ? Perhaps we could meet after lunch today, when I trust we will be able to let you have our decision.'

Karen gathered up her papers and put them back into her black leather document case. Arnold picked up his own from the floor and followed her out of the room. In the corridor outside she expelled her breath noisily. 'Bloody hell! I'm glad that's over. No more having to toady around that disgusting little man.' She flashed him a quick glance. 'Arnold, I need a drink. To hell with the group meetings. Lead me somewhere, out of here. Now.'

They left their document cases at the reception desk and walked out of the hotel towards the cour d'honneur. They sat in the sunshine at a small cafe. As he ordered drinks Karen looked up appreciatively at the surrounding buildings.

'Romanesque at the lower tier,' Arnold advised, 'Gothic in the middle, Renaissance above.'

She fixed him with a long, contemplative glance, and shook her head. 'You can be very boring, you know,' she complained. 'I was just thinking how romantic all this was.'

She was different. The strict formality of their relationship in the office, the tensions, the competitiveness and distrust that seemed a normal concomitant of their relationship, seemed to have been dissipated. She was much more relaxed. He liked the change. It meant that possibly they might even get around to talking about what had happened during the riots at Alnwick. It lay between them, a bridge to be crossed. He watched her profile as she sighed, closed her eyes, raised her face to the sun. He leaned forward, about to raise the matter.

The waiter arrived. '*Gin tonic, m' sieur. Et un cognac. Merci.*'

She opened her eyes. 'How do you reckon our chances, Arnold?' she asked.

She was not talking about their relationship. The moment had gone. They sat in the sunshine and talked about professional things.

* * *

After lunch they attended the afternoon conference session, which consisted of a presentation by a geophysical expert on recent developments in survey techniques. Arnold was soon somewhat lost as the earnest young man talked of magnetometer surveys, resistivity and magnetic susceptibilities. He looked around him. The session was being chaired by a member of the local Nimes branch of the FCAI, the members of the FCAI committee were notable by their absence. Arnold guessed they would be in session, discussing the proposals put forward by Karen Stannard in her first interview with James Stead.

The afternoon dragged on. There was a break for tea, and then another less than exciting presentation from a Scandinavian speaker whose heavy accent was difficult to decipher. There was a scattering of muted applause at his conclusion, Karen touched Arnold's arm. He looked at her; she nodded towards the back of the room.

James Stead was standing there. As he caught sight of them he raised a hand, made a drinking motion. They got the message. Karen rose and Arnold followed her. They made their way to the bar. James Stead was already there with a gin and tonic in his hand. He drained it as they joined him, and as they did so Julian Mwate, Charles Midgley and Martin Woudt also entered the bar.

'This looks momentous . . . maybe even some kind of celebration.' Karen suggested warily.

James Stead beamed. 'It is, as far as you're concerned.'

'You've reached a decision already?'

'The chairman has been quite persuasive.' Julian Mwate commented, with a sly glance at Arnold.

'But the committee were unanimous,' Stead insisted. 'Though I will admit that Karen's discussions with me, and her presentation, have made me a strong supporter of the project. The good news, my dear,' he said, addressing the woman who had clearly bewitched him, and touching her lightly on the arm, 'is that the committee has decided to support the Fordbridge project. I am unable to state at this point the extent of the financial investment we might make, because as I'm sure you'll be aware we are a committee only, and we have to report back to the Holborn Trust. However, I have already been in touch with the chairman of trustees, and I am fairly confident . . . there has never previously been any difficulty in acceptance of our committee recommendations.'

'So congratulations would seem to be in order,' Charles Midgley suggested.

A bottle of champagne had appeared, the glasses were distributed. The group moved to chairs in the far corner of the bar. 'The rest of the conference members will be arriving soon and we'll get rather crowded in here, so perhaps I'd better give you some details of our proposals,' James Stead announced. 'First of all we, as a committee, will be recommending a significant financial support for the project. Hopefully, it will be sufficient for the work to be largely completed before the property developer reaches his deadline.'

'That's excellent news — and we're grateful,' Karen replied, flashing a smile around the group.

James Stead blinked and a shadow of disappointment touched his eyes. He had clearly hoped such a smile would be reserved for him alone.

'But while the financial support will arrive without strings, we're also of the opinion that the work would be able to proceed with greater despatch,' James went on, 'if we were able to get your agreement — it is your project after all — that suitable members of this committee should also be encouraged to play a central role in the investigation.'

Karen glanced uncertainly at Arnold, then nodded carefully, considering the suggestion. 'Of course, we're short of manpower and expertise, and if we can enlist the assistance of suitable people—'

'For instance,' Stead rumbled, waving his champagne glass generously in Charles Midgley's direction, 'While Professor Forray is unfortunately unavailable because of commitments at the Sorbonne, we have our distinguished forensic scientist here in Dr Midgley. I'm sure he'd welcome the opportunity to look more closely at the skeleton remains of the woman interred at Fordbridge.'

'I can't give too much time,' Midgley commented. 'I'm pretty busy with a backlog at the labs, but I'd very much like to be involved. Put in what time I can.'

'And Charles is based in the north-east which helps. As is our friend Dr Mwate.' Stead added.

The big Zimbabwean nodded. His lips drew back in a broad smile as he beamed at Karen Stannard. 'I've already mentioned to Arnold that I intended approaching you through formal university channels, about helping out with the research into the shamanic drawings at the Abbey Head sea cave. He's mentioned possible links with the chariot burial. So, if it would be welcome, I'd like to liaise closely with your group, at both Abbey Head and Fordbridge, and help out where I can. I'll have research students at the university, in addition . . .'

Karen inclined her head in graceful acknowledgement. 'We'd love to have you involved, Dr Mwate.'

'And then there's Martin,' James Stead continued. 'Since he's based in Amsterdam there might be a little more difficulty in his involvement with the project—'

Martin Woudt's pale eyes glistened and he shook his head. 'Difficulties that are not insuperable, I assure you. I am well used to travelling to the north-east. There is the ferry to Hull, from Rotterdam. It is an easy crossing. And the short distance from Hull to Newcastle . . . it is not a problem. I also would welcome involvement.'

'Gentlemen,' Karen announced, raising her champagne glass, 'I'm delighted. I look forward to a close cooperation.'

'My only regret,' James Stead suggested, 'is that I personally will not be involved. But I'm sure, as project overseer, I will be able to find time to call on you from time to time, Karen, to see how things are progressing.'

Arnold had no doubt about it.

The group remained there, finishing the champagne. James Stead called for another bottle, shifted his seat closer to Karen to engage her in more private discussion, and shortly afterwards the members of the conference began to stream in. The bar became crowded, and the small party split up as others came across to raise various matters about the conference organization, and discuss details arising out of the papers presented in full session. Arnold noted how there was a noticeable surge of males wishing to talk over matters with Karen Stannard. He doubted that they were all motivated by the elegance of her presentation.

His mind drifted back to the thoughts that had occupied him. Back at the office, he'd had the idea that Carcassonne might be an opportunity for Karen and himself to have a personal discussion, to determine how they might progress in a professional relationship that was often rocky, and a personal relationship that had become confusing and difficult. He realized now that such a chance was unlikely. More relaxed and flushed with success she might be, but the opportunity for the two of them to have a private discussion seemed remote.

He glanced at his watch: it was perhaps an hour and a half to dinner. In common with some of the group he'd left his FCAI document case on one of the settees near the bar. He retrieved it now, made his apologies and slipped away from the noisy, convivial group.

He went back to his room, threw the document case on the bed, stripped and took a shower. He lay on the bed for a while, thinking about missed opportunities. He dressed slowly, changing for dinner. He glanced at his watch, decided there'd be time for a brief walk in the fresh air before they all congregated in the dining room. He was heading for the door when the bedside telephone rang.

'Arnold?'

He recognized the voice immediately. 'Karen.'

'Can you help a lady in potential trouble?'

'What's the problem?' he asked warily.

There was a short pause, and then a low, throaty chuckle. 'Don't sound so cagey. To put it bluntly, I think that our revered chairman of the FCAI, who has pushed through a decision in our favour, will be expecting, shall we say, a quid pro quo at some stage this evening. Ordinarily, I wouldn't see that as a problem. I can handle myself. But, in the circumstances, here in Carcassonne . . . I'd rather not face the challenge. There are better ways to spend the evening.'

'What do you want me to do?'

'Skip dinner, take me out and show me the illuminations. As promised.'

His hesitation was brief. 'It'll be my pleasure.'

'I'll be ready in ten minutes.'

Arnold replaced the phone, sat down on the edge of the bed. He was unable to deny the slow surge of excitement in his veins. It could be that Karen was telling the truth about wanting to avoid an embarrassing interview with James Stead; on the other hand, maybe her comments about Stead were at least in part an excuse. He remembered the way she had hesitated in the doorway of his office back in Morpeth, had seemed to be about to say something about their relationship. He took a deep breath. He was not certain what to think.

He rose, prowled around his room edgily. He knew he'd have to be careful this evening. It could so easily be ruined, because he was still unable to determine just what made Karen Stannard tick. He remembered all the office gossip about her, that she was really not interested in men. He recalled his own feelings, all those occasions when she had deliberately cut him down, humiliated him, made his professional life difficult, challenged him when she saw him as a threat to her own professional position. But also, the memory of the evening in Alnwick came back, when she had been injured in the racist riot, had been vulnerable, and they had spent the night together. He had left early next morning, uncertain how to handle the situation. She had never referred to it since. Nor had he.

Tonight, things might be different.

His glance fell upon the document case on his bed. He picked it up, intending to place it on the desk in front of the window. Then he paused. It felt different, somehow. It was heavier, thicker in its contents than he had anticipated.

He realized suddenly that it was not his. He had picked up the wrong document case. It was a mistake easy to make. All delegates had received similar leather cases as a gift from the FCAI. They had all been crowded in the bar. He and others had placed their cases down. He tried to recall who had been sitting near him when they had been enjoying the champagne. He could not recall with precision.

He hesitated, toyed with the document case, then slowly opened it. There might be some clue inside to enable him to identify its owner. There were various papers inside; handouts to support the lectures given in the conference, but everyone had received those, and they provided no clue to the identity of the owner.

The thick envelope nestling among the conference papers was certainly not his. It had no superscription. He thought about it for a moment, then opened the envelope, which was unsealed, and drew out the contents. He stared at them for several seconds, and something cold turned in his stomach. The telephone rang.

'Arnold? I'm ready. See you downstairs.'

Slowly he put the photographs back into the envelope, pushed the envelope back into the document case. There was a dead feeling in his lower stomach as he walked towards the lift. Karen was waiting for him in the lobby downstairs.

She looked stunning. She was wearing a simple dress, but it clung to her figure, outlining the swing of her hips, and the low neckline emphasized the swell of her breasts. Her hair was loose and seemed to glow. Her eyes sparkled as she held out her hand to him. He thought she had never looked more beautiful. 'So,' she murmured, 'show me the town.'

He strolled with her into the heart of La Cité and she linked her arm into his, leaning against him as they walked. She was relaxed, conscious of a job well done. She chattered in an inconsequential way as he had never heard her talk before. She seemed to be excited about the town itself, moved by the warm night and the sky full of bright stars.

They found a small restaurant where they could be seated in a garden open to that sky, with muted lamplight glittering among arching jacaranda trees and heavily loaded vines, candles glowing and flickering on their damask-clothed table. The wine was excellent, the seafood fresh, the ambience all they could have wished for. The conference was behind them, the office in Morpeth was a world away, and he had never seen her so relaxed, so exuberant, so poised. He was aware that the eyes of other male diners were drawn to her, but he knew also he was a poor companion. He tried to match her mood but found it impossible.

All he could think of was the photographs in the document case.

He tried to dismiss them, but they were there in the front of his mind. He thought the wine would help, and drank freely, but his conversation was stilted, and gradually her own excitement at her success with the FCAI, being here in Carcassonne, under the stars, enjoying a good meal, began to fade.

Finally, she asked him, 'Is something the matter?'

He didn't feel he could tell her. He was still confused, uncertain what to do. He shook his head, tried to recover the situation, but his reserve made her own attitude change and she became cooler. They finished their meal and she looked at him reflectively. Her eyes were dark and deep in the candlelight. 'Okay. You told me the illuminated Cité was quite a sight. You going to show me?'

She allowed him to pay the bill. He walked with her through the narrow streets, past the church of St Gimer, towards the west gateway. Ahead of them, the lights of the Ville Basse were spread wide. At the Pont Vieux he paused, and they looked back. The fortified medieval stronghold was above them, outlined against the evening sky, its crenelations and towers and battlements lit by the spotlights directed to their tall walls. They leaned back against massive stones still warm from the day's sun and she was standing close to him. She raised her head, looked up to the high walls, illuminated by cleverly located spotlights. 'It's magnificent,' she sighed.

Her bare shoulder touched his. He knew suddenly that if he turned, her face would be close to his. He remembered the way they had kissed, that one night in Alnwick. The woman he had known as hard and committed and distrustful, competitive in her attitude towards him, had been different that night. As she was now.

But it was no good.

She was reserved as they walked back through the narrow streets to their hotel, saying little. When they entered the hotel she walked straight towards the lift. He stepped in beside her but as it ascended she said nothing. Her goodnight was short and casual. He cursed himself and went back to his room.

The document case was still there, on his bed.

His mind churned on, still trying to recall, as he had been doing all evening, just who had been standing close to him in the bar, seated beside him, exactly who might have placed his document case down on the bar settee, to be confused with his while they stood there drinking, congratulating themselves.

He thought back but it was all hazy, so many people around. And yet, logically, it could be only one person. The contents pointed that way, if the worst was not to be believed. Slowly, he tore off a sheet from the telephone pad beside his bed. He wrote a short note.

Sorry. I picked your case up by mistake.
AL

He took the document case, walked down to reception. There was no one there, but the hotel register was on the desk. He opened it, checked the names quickly, found the room number. He took the lift back up to the third floor. He rang the bell, hesitated, but then his courage failed him. Embarrassed, he placed the document case on the floor outside the room, leaning it against the door, and left.

He slept badly, tossing and turning on the bed, thinking of Karen and a ruined evening. He had the feeling that he'd left himself in a situation, as far as their personal relationship was concerned, from which he might never recover.

2

The overnight storm that had caused havoc in the North Sea and left a Norwegian freighter wallowing helplessly off Amble had abated somewhat by morning, but there were radio warnings of continuing high winds, and the rain had not ceased, a relentless driving rain that was sweeping in from the north-east. The weather served to further dampen DCI O'Connor's spirits. He had left an interview with Sid Cathery angry and annoyed, because the Assistant Chief Constable had again refused to permit further manpower to be drafted in to assist with the headless torso case. DI Farnsby had also been present at the meeting, and O'Connor suspected that he had some sympathy with O'Connor, for he himself had expressed a certain frustration at his continued responsibility for the car smuggling operation working out of South Shields, a task he clearly considered lacking in priority. But O'Connor had not had the opportunity to discuss the matter with Farnsby. He was already late for a scheduled meeting in his own office.

The two men he was expecting were already there when he arrived. They had been given cups of coffee but were obviously not impressed by the standard of the canteen refreshment. Both cups were standing on O'Connor's desk, cooling, barely touched. There was a warm, steamy atmosphere in the office. The windows were tightly closed against the lashing rain and two raincoats hanging behind the door were dripping steadily on the carpet.

'Bloody weather,' O'Connor said as he entered the room.

'Is that why you're late?' Charles Midgley asked, with a hint of irritation in his voice.

O'Connor shook his head. 'Meeting with the ACC.'

'Constructive?'

O'Connor rolled his eyes but said nothing. Midgley laughed, his annoyance at being kept waiting dissipated. He had met Cathery and would no doubt have formed his own opinion. O'Connor turned to Midgley's companion. 'I guess you must be Dr Mwate.'

'The same.' The big black man flashed white teeth and extended his hand; his grip was hard, his hand massive. He topped O'Connor by several inches, his bulk was impressive.

'So,' Charles Midgley began, settling back in his chair. 'How are things going with the investigation into the boy's killing?'

O'Connor sat down with a sigh and ran a frustrated hand over his face. 'Don't ask. If I was talking to the press I'd be more discreet, but since you're almost family, so to speak, I can tell you we're getting bloody nowhere.' He scowled at the forensic scientist. 'We can't find a starting point, for God's sake. If we could only get some leads from you people, something to go on—'

Midgley was displeased by the implied rebuke and shook his head. 'I know the kind of stuff you'd like to hear, but you've got to realize, DCI, we've run all kinds of tests on the body but we've so little to go on. Have *you* got anywhere with the tartan shorts?'

O'Connor scratched his head irritably. 'We've run the information you gave us through the computer, and we've checked with manufacturers. The brand has been determined — Kidwear — and we know there's a firm selling the stuff through outlets in the UK. But it seems the UK firm is operating under a licence from a European firm, and as far as can be determined, it seems the shorts were not made in the UK, though there is the likelihood they were distributed here. Which is a big help! It means we've now got to drag our way through all the UK outlets, but also do a trawl throughout the Continent, and God knows where else to find some kind of match.'

'How will you do that?' Dr Mwate enquired.

'Interpol,' O'Connor replied. 'They have a database. That's all they are really, a bloody big database. An information centre. Not what the public assumes. But if Interpol do come up with a match, saying the item was made, say, in Germany, where the hell does that take us? The kid was killed here, that's for sure, so it's a problem for our jurisdiction.'

'So you've no leads, no theories you can follow up?' Midgley asked, frowning.

O'Connor shrugged. 'Where the hell do we start? Why would someone cut off a kid's head and limbs? What's so important about the identification? What was the motive for the killing in the first place? No, the damned annoying and frustrating thing is, we just don't know where to begin. It's an investigative black hole, believe me!'

'Have you considered bringing in a psychological profiler?' Dr Mwate asked tentatively.

O'Connor shook his head. 'I know that the current fashion is to believe such guys can point the finger unerringly at the likely killer. Intellectual supermen; magical diviners. But there's no point in even considering it here. With the amount of information we've got — *concrete* information I mean — what could we give a profiler? There just isn't enough information to allow him to build up a psychological profile of the man who did this thing.'

The forensic scientist leaned back in his chair and glanced at Dr Mwate. He pinched his nostrils between finger and thumb, frowning thoughtfully. 'I realized that this was what things would be like. It's why I suggested you might like to talk to my friend here.'

O'Connor glanced at Dr Mwate, taking in the broad shoulders, the sheer size of the man. He would have made a good beat copper, he thought to himself. Instead, he was a university professor. You could never go by appearances. He turned, responded to Dr Midgley. 'I'm not sure just how Dr Mwate can help, but when you have no theories to work on, any theory has to be considered.'

There was a slight smile on Mwate's lips. His eyes gleamed. 'Even the most fanciful and terrible theories?'

'I'm here to listen,' O'Connor rejoined. 'I have what you might describe as an open mind. Empty even. So fire away.'

Mwate hesitated, and glanced at Midgley as though for guidance. The forensic scientist nodded encouragingly. Mwate locked his powerful fingers together and nodded. 'I understand that no person has come forward to report a disappearance.'

'None that matches the torso we have in the labs.'

'And you've come up with no rational reason that would suggest a necessity for the removal of head and limbs?'

'Other than to prevent identification, no.'

'But what if the removal had little — or nothing — to do with the process of identification? What if the head and limbs were removed for other reasons?' Mwate asked slowly, a frown on his face.

O'Connor watched him for a little while, thinking. He glanced at Midgley, who was listening intently. O'Connor chewed at his lip. 'When Dr Midgley contacted me, and mentioned your name, he suggested that all this might have something to do with the origins of the boy. The fact he was African. But I didn't quite follow . . .'

'Dr Mwate has done some research in Africa, concerning the use and relevance of traditional medicinal practices in the active suppression of AIDS in the continent,' Midgley intervened. 'You're probably aware that some politicians deny the existence of HIV, or claim it's all a Western-devised plot to recolonize Africa. You may also be aware that in the villages, in the bush, there is a tendency to distrust and turn away from modern medical practices to seek remedies within the tribal or village group.'

'The research was not actually undertaken by me,' Mwate demurred in a soft tone. 'It was under my supervision, at the university in Zimbabwe. But . . . certain unpleasant facts came to light in that research.'

O'Connor frowned. 'Involving decapitation?'

Mwate shrugged. 'Not simply that. But we're talking about the rejection of qualified doctors and modern hospitals here. The practice of *umu thi*, or *muti* in short, is well spread throughout the African continent. In essence, it's a largely harmless reliance upon traditional herbal medicines, some of which are effective, having been used for centuries, if not millennia. After all, many of our modern medicines come from everyday natural matter, such as tree bark for instance. And it involves a belief in the effectiveness of ritual.'

There was a short silence. Slowly, O'Connor asked, 'I don't understand. What has this got to do with the matter in hand? Are you suggesting the boy was involved in some sort of ritual killing?'

Mwate frowned and shook his head. 'No . . . it's something rather more . . . well, just seems to me that maybe the practice of *muti* is involved here.'

'You said it was just harmless traditional medicine,' O'Connor objected.

'That's true, generally. But there is considerable evidence to suggest it's also become associated with a macabre trade throughout Nigeria, Zambia, Zimbabwe and South Africa.'

'Trade?'

'It's a trade in human body parts.' Mwate said quietly, his red-rimmed eyes fixed sombrely on O'Connor.

There was a short silence. The rain seemed to have eased a little, ceased its drumming against the window. 'Who the hell would trade in body parts?' O'Connor asked. 'They're used by *sangomas*.'

'Witch doctors?' O'Connor said in surprise.

'You've heard of them?'

'I've read Rider Haggard. Gagool, the ancient smeller-out of victims in *King Solomon's Mines*. All that sort of stuff. But what would they use the body parts for?'

Mwate's dark brow was furrowed. 'The *sangomas* make so-called life-giving potions out of them, or cures for various illnesses.'

'That's barbaric.' O'Connor snapped, shocked in spite of himself.

'Traditional,' Mwate demurred. 'You see, belief in the power of such medicines is widespread in African tradition. It's not dissimilar from the kind of logic that suggests that strength comes from removing the heart of a respected enemy, from wearing the skin of a dead leopard or eating the flesh of a lion. By such an action you can assume the swiftness of the leopard, the power of the biggest of cats, the strength of a powerful opponent. Similarly, among the *sangomas*, and the people who go to them for help, the medical use of human body parts is regarded as especially powerful. For instance, I've come across a severed hand being buried at the entrance to a shop.'

'What the hell was the point of that?' O'Connor asked in amazement.

'Believe it or not, the object was to encourage trade. Powerful medicine, to bring good luck to the shop concerned.' Mwate paused, staring at O'Connor, recognizing the shadows of disbelief in his eyes. 'You might think it far-fetched, crazy maybe, but we're talking about deep-seated beliefs among backward, primitive minds. It's much more common to find that the body parts are mixed with other ingredients, and smeared all over the body in the form of an ointment, or medicine.' His tone deepened, his voice dropping. 'Sometimes the pieces of flesh are cooked in a stew. For human consumption.'

O'Connor's stomach growled in slow complaint. He leaned back in his chair, folded his arms, slightly nauseated. He thought of the torso in the river. 'Does this apply to all parts of the body . . . this medicine thing?'

'All human parts are imbued with medicinal value in *muti*,' Mwate replied gravely. 'But the genitals of young boys, and the labia of young virgin girls, these are especially prized.' His eyes were cold. 'Their harvesting and sale is a particularly lucrative business.'

'And you say the practice is widespread in Africa?' Mwate shrugged. 'It's impossible to say how many missing people in Africa have been murdered for their body parts. But a report of the South African Witchcraft Commission believes that a significant proportion of children reported as missing have been killed in *muti* murders every year.'

'But why children in particular?' O'Connor queried, shaking his head.

'The body parts of children are considered more valuable, because they are uncontaminated by previous sexual activity.' Mwate spread his large hands and sighed. 'They are thus regarded as pure, and more potent.'

'And this is still happening in Africa?' O'Connor asked in disbelief.

'DCI O'Connor, it was only last year that a *sangoma* was prosecuted in Malawi for killing an eleven-year-old boy. The child's body was found with the heart and stomach removed. The *sangoma* had sold these parts, with the assurance that consumption of the body parts would bring strength and virility to his elderly patient, and enable him to have further children, with his young new wife. There's no doubt the practice is widespread, but I should stress we're only talking here about the fringes of society, the uneducated, the people still gripped by primitive beliefs.'

'But you're not really talking about Africa, you're suggesting that these ideas may have come here,' O'Connor considered.

Mwate regarded him gravely. 'Not may. From what I have heard regarding the killing of this African boy, I would say they almost certainly have.'

There was a silence in the room, broken only by the rain recommencing its attack, lashing violently against the window. At last, Dr Midgley cleared his throat, and said, 'Since we were unable to discover, in the labs, any obvious evidence of sexual abuse, it remains a mystery why someone felt the need to murder and mutilate a small boy in such a grotesque manner. The mutilation . . . we've been proceeding along the line that it was probably motivated by a desire to prevent identification. What Dr Mwate is suggesting is that there might have been another, quite different reason. It opens up . . . another line of enquiry.'

O'Connor felt vaguely dizzy. 'But selling body parts, here in the north-east . . . I can hardly credit it.'

Mwate wrinkled his brow. 'It's not really so incredible. We have recently read of cases of doctors here in England who have been struck off by the British Medical Council because they have been caught offering for sale body parts from Middle Eastern donors.'

'Hell, I know that trade exists! But they were hearts, and lungs, destined for transplant purposes.'

Mwate shrugged. 'If for transplant, why not for other purposes? Body parts can be sought for other uses by desperate people — if they have a belief in the efficacy of the treatment.'

O'Connor stared at Dr Mwate, saw the sombreness in his eyes, heard the belief in his tones. There was solid logic in the argument, even if the possibilities he raised made O'Connor's flesh creep.

It was difficult to take a detached stance in respect of the murder of the boy. Mwate's suggestions had left a bad taste in O'Connor's mouth, and there was a barely subdued rage growing in him. He wanted to get his hands on the killer of the boy, but he knew it was necessary to retain his focus, determine his priorities. The theory that Mwate had propounded gave them a new line of enquiry and one that he would have to pursue, but when he saw the fascinated horror and disbelief in the faces of his team, when he called them to a case conference later in the day, he knew that they would all find it difficult to concentrate in face of such an outlandish theory, and one beyond their previous experience.

And there was also the problem of political correctness. He could imagine the howls of rage and protest that would arise in certain parts of the community minorities if he started a hunt for witch doctor practices and beliefs. He did not report to Sid Cathery on the matter. He suspected the ACC would have strong views on the subject.

And there was still the essential line to follow, it was something he stressed to the team. 'We still have to find out who the boy was, before we can find out who did this to him. And we will, even if we don't know how long it will take . . .'

After his case conference he made his disconsolate way to the canteen. Farnsby was already there, seated alone in the corner of the room. O'Connor obtained a coffee for himself, hesitated, then went across to the DI's table. 'Mind if I join you?'

Farnsby looked up. His expression confirmed that he clearly found the intrusion unwelcome. He said nothing for a moment, then shrugged. 'Free country.'

They sat silently for a little while, O'Connor making no attempt to begin a conversation. Farnsby looked up eventually, curious in spite of himself. 'You seem down in the dumps.'

'I could say it was the weather.'

'But it isn't. Getting nowhere with the African boy's case?'

'Let's say we're bloody short of leads.'

Farnsby was hesitant. He said nothing for a while. Then he grunted. 'There's been a rumour going around HQ that you're calling in Interpol. That mean you think the boy could have been killed outside the country?'

O'Connor shook his head. 'No, I don't think that can be the case. Time scales are against it: the kid was in the river for a few days only. And it's surely inconceivable that a killer would run the risk of transporting a murdered child abroad . . .' O'Connor sipped noisily at his coffee and pulled a face. 'God, it doesn't get any better, does it? Talking of transportation, how is your case going?'

Farnsby's mouth twisted, he took a deep breath. 'I'm taking it slowly. I've been working through the files. I think

72

the whole thing was really cocked up in the first instance. This guy Catford, there's a lot of suspicion about him and if the pressure had really been put on at the time, maybe something would have stuck.'

'He'd been shipping stolen cars into Europe?'

'That's the suspicion. But he was friendly with a couple of businessmen in Newcastle, they talked to the chief constable, and somehow, it was just one of those cases that the Old Man got pulled.'

'Do you think the Chief was getting backhanders?' O'Connor asked curiously.

Farnsby shrugged. 'Who knows? He was forced into early retirement, but he never confided in me — blue-eyed boy or not,' he added bitterly.

'So where do you go from here?' O'Connor asked, ignoring the resentment.

'I'll be doing what Mr Cathery wants. I've managed to dig out a bit about Catford's history . . . His path crossed the ACC's when Cathery was with the Somerset Police. Smuggling: cigarettes, booze and drugs. Seems Cathery got a bit obsessive about the case, stuck his neck out, pushed too hard for a conviction. It blew up in his face. No case to answer. There was some hint of manufactured evidence, or illegally obtained information. And Catford screamed blue murder about it, even brought a suit for harassment, and claimed the drugs were planted by one of Cathery's minions. It was all settled out of court in the end. Cathery had to back down, got an official reprimand. He's never forgotten it. So now, even after all these years, he wants blood. Seeing Catford's name on a file up here, it was like throwing fish to a seal. Cathery was up in a moment, honking and clapping his flippers.'

The image lightened O'Connor's spirits, and he chuckled. 'So what's next?'

Farnsby grimaced in distaste. 'So, I'll be doing what the boss wants. I'll be paying a visit to Mr Don Catford next week, see what I can do to stir things up.'

O'Connor stared at his coffee, considering matters. Carefully, he asked, 'Why don't I come along with you?'

The silence that followed was frosty. Farnsby's gaze was fixed firmly on the table in front of him, his saturnine features still. 'I don't know that's a good idea.'

'Look,' O'Connor said earnestly, 'I think we got off to a bad start, you and me. I can understand the way you've been feeling, about me coming into Culpeper's job when you thought it was lined up for you. And then there was the ACC pulling you off the Starlight Club business. But that's no reason for us to keep our distance. I had no part in the ACC's decision. And I applied for this job without any view about the situation here.'

Farnsby struggled with the argument, unwilling to accept it. 'You've got your own hands full enough with the torso case,' he muttered sullenly.

'Hell, I could do with a break from it! Get some fresh new air, down at South Shields.'

'I don't need any help on a piddling job like this one.'

'Hey, two pair of eyes and hands are always better than one!' O'Connor persisted. 'Maybe we could wrap up the Catford business faster. Get you on to something more worthwhile. Maybe bring you in on the torso murder. Believe me, I need the bloody assistance.'

'What about the ACC?' Farnsby asked, warily.

'He doesn't check our work schedules. What's it got to do with him, as long as we do the business?'

O'Connor knew the detective inspector was unconvinced and unwilling, still distrustful. As Farnsby remained silent, O'Connor saw Detective Sergeant Robinson enter the canteen. The thickset, burly officer bought himself a chocolate bar and a packet of biscuits at the counter. As he turned away and headed past them towards the door O'Connor called out to him. 'Big lad like you ought to watch what he's eating!'

Robinson hesitated. 'Got to keep the belly-fires burning.' He glanced at Farnsby, digested the fact they were seated together. 'Council of war?'

'Trying to pass a peace pipe more like,' O'Connor replied. 'Here, park that big backside of yours for a while.'

Robinson hesitated, his heavy features doubtful. 'Can't really. I got an interview to conduct . . . but maybe a few minutes.'

He sat down. O'Connor shifted his chair so he could face the big man. 'So how's the Starlight interviews going?'

Robinson shot an uneasy glance at Farnsby, then shrugged. 'It's a bugger. My guess is these guys really don't know who set up the website. We've got the group bang to rights, we've built the case and they know it, so they've got nothing to lose by giving up this guy, but they're still not doing it. I really think they don't know who The Doctor is.'

Farnsby raised his head, curious in spite of his resentment at being removed from the investigation. 'No way through the computer files? No hints of his location?'

Robinson shook his head. 'We've been trawling through the files, the experts have got into the hard drives, they're throwing all sort of mucky stuff up, making links with European networks, digging even deeper holes for the guys we got in the cells, but The Doctor . . . who the hell he is, we're no closer to finding out. We'll nail these other bastards, the ones we've got, no doubt about that. Even the CPS are convinced we can send them down in quick time. But the other guy we really want, The Doctor . . .'

'Well, if there's anything we can do to help,' O'Connor said easily.

Robinson looked surprised. He glanced at Farnsby, uncertainly. 'Yeah, well, that's good. Maybe I'll take you up on that.' He glanced at his watch. 'Hey, I've got to go.'

He rose, unwrapped his chocolate bar and began to nibble at it as he marched across the room and out of the canteen. O'Connor watched him go, then turned back to Farnsby. The detective inspector was staring at him. Some of the dark-visaged petulance seemed to have drained from his features. Hesitantly, he said, 'I think maybe you could be right.'

'About what?'

Farnsby took a deep breath. 'I think maybe I've been . .. overreacting. The fact is, I've been working in Culpeper's shadow for more than a few years and it hasn't been easy.'

'He was difficult to work with?'

Farnsby was surprisingly reluctant to agree with the comment. He twisted his mouth, grimaced. 'Well, yes, I have to say he was. He gave me hell at times. But looking back, I'm not sure the problem lay only with him — and I had my own problems too. You see, Culpeper was one of the old school. I've no doubt he resented my relatively rapid promotion to detective inspector. He'd come up the hard way, slogging it on the beat. I was spared much of that. But you have to agree that he knew Tyneside like the back of his hairy hand; he'd — well, served his time, you know what I mean?'

'But you still didn't get on with him.' O'Connor said quietly.

'That's right, but it wasn't because he was wrong.' Farnsby's eyes were clouded with reluctantly dredged memories. 'He sort of had his way of working and I had mine. I suppose I was all for the quick fix, whereas he . . . he tended to say, hey, I've been there, son, tried that, it didn't work . . . I found that irritating. But when you come down to it, now he's gone . . . I look back and I think maybe it was just a clash of temperament, nothing much more than that. I wanted to dash off to prove a case; he used to say hold on, let me think about it, there's a file somewhere . . .'

'And was there?' O'Connor asked curiously.

Farnsby managed a wry smile. 'Not really. Except in his head. The fact is, he knew a lot of people on Tyneside, kept tag on the villains from way back. He'd had the kind of upbringing in the force that meant he had a lot of history in his head. The files, yes, there'd be occasions when he could dig something out, dust off some papers, turn up something other people had forgotten about. But most of it was there in that thick skull of his. It sometimes took some digging out, believe me . . . but the old bugger could be impressive, the way he remembered things. And sometimes . . . damned right.'

Farnsby took a sip of his coffee and was silent for a little while. At last he looked fiercely at O'Connor and asked, 'You meant what you said earlier? Pipe of peace?'

'Seems the sensible way to go forward,' O'Connor replied easily.

'I think maybe I'll go along with that.' Farnsby's glance was level. 'And to hell with the ACC.'

'I'll drink to that,' O'Connor laughed.

'And I'd welcome your coming along when I go to see this guy Catford. On one condition.'

O'Connor knew already what was coming. 'You'll be the guy in charge.'

'Exactly that.'

O'Connor extended his hand. 'Deal,' he said.

Surprised at the gesture, Farnsby hesitated, then grasped O'Connor's hand. 'Truce?' he said.

'Truce,' DCI O'Connor agreed.

But coming to terms with Farnsby still did nothing to prevent the worms crawling in his mind, worms put there by Dr Julian Mwate and his suggestions of another motive for the decapitation of the young African boy. On the other hand, something Farnsby had said rang some bells with O'Connor.

Maybe he should take time to look up retired Detective Chief Inspector Culpeper.

3

The recent thunderstorms sweeping in from the North Sea had left the site at Fordbridge awash to some extent, with long-dormant springs bursting from the slope and muddy puddles swamping part of the area at the foot of the hill, but the team had taken the precaution of erecting shelters of canvas over the main excavations. Consequently, although the day was still grey, under hurried, scudding clouds, work was able to proceed, even though fingers were chilled with the wind cutting in from the sea.

Dr Martin Woudt had arrived at the site with Arnold, who introduced him to the staff working there and showed him the main areas of excavation. When he had been given a preliminary look at the dig, Arnold took him to the hut which had been erected on site where some of the artefacts were being labelled, noted and given a preliminary washing. Thereafter they would be transferred to the labs for processing with the cartwheels that were being cut from their soil blocks and subjected to a close analysis.

Woudt demonstrated considerable interest in what he was seeing. His narrow eyes gleamed enthusiastically, and his features were more than normally animated. 'The site is rather more extensive than I had appreciated. There seem to be most interesting opportunities to be grasped here.' He spent a considerable time inspecting the burial pit which was still being excavated under a plastic tent, exclaimed over the foundations of the medieval manorial complex that had first led them to the cart burial, and handled the iron lynchpins and nave hoops with care, peering at the evidence of bronze sheeting. He joined Arnold in the entrance of the hut, rubbing his slender hands, and nodded in the direction of the houses that were going up lower down the hill. 'This is where Mr Holderness is building his housing estate, I see.'

'That's right,' Arnold replied. 'And as you'll notice, the roadway is creeping up the hill. It's quite clear Joe Holderness will want us off his land by the end of the three months.'

Woudt smiled thinly, somewhat fastidiously brushing dirt and mud from his slimly tapered hands. 'Your Miss Stannard was not able to persuade him? I was under the impression she could charm . . . as you say, birds from the trees.'

If they were male, Arnold thought. He glanced at Martin Woudt. He had the vague impression that the Dutch professor from the Rijksmuseum was somehow impervious to Karen Stannard's sexuality. It was a thought that had occurred to him that morning, when he had been called into Karen Stannard's office.

'It seems things are moving fast,' she had said abruptly when he entered her room. 'Dr Woudt is due in this morning. I get the impression he's bringing us a formal confirmation of the agreement by the trustees of the Holborn Trust. They're going to accept the recommendation of the FCAI committee — which means we're in business. Do you think we can finish the work in time?'

'I think we're now in with a chance,' he replied optimistically.

There was a hint of glowing excitement in her eyes; her movements were animated, her breathing quick. But any hints there might have been of a relaxation in their relationship in Carcassonne were now dissipated. The softness, the invitation had gone from her glance. She was now back to her own business-orientated, professional self. It was as though the vulnerability of Alnwick, and in a way, Carcassonne too, had been discarded, memories obliterated. To a certain extent Arnold felt relieved. He felt he was now on familiar, safer ground, knew where he stood. He could forget the uncertainties of the last week. He could concentrate on tasks in hand.

She was staring at him, one elegant eyebrow raised quizzically. 'Do you think you can handle Dr Woudt?' she asked abruptly.

'How do you mean?'

'He'll want to go out to take a look at the Fordbridge site. Ordinarily I'd have gone with him. If only to cement the deal, make sure no feathers were ruffled before we get a firm commitment from the FCAI. But I think it might be better if you took him out there.'

'I'm happy to do so,' Arnold hesitated. 'But in view of the importance of the financial support we're likely to get from the FCAI, he might be a bit . . . put out if he doesn't get the attention of the head of the department.'

She observed him carefully, suspicious that he might be insincere in his comment. She shook her head, leaned forward on her desk, touched one slim finger to her lips indecisively. 'I don't know. You have a point, but . . . well, I find Dr Martin Woudt hard work. He's something of a cold fish.'

'In what way?'

'He doesn't seem to relate to me too well,' she said soberly.

He raised his eyebrows. 'He doesn't come across to me as a misogynist.'

She smiled. 'I didn't say he was. Socially, he reacts well enough. We had a few chats in Carcassonne, outside the conference. But . . . I'm left with a certain feeling . . . well, let's say I think maybe we'll get more mileage out of the situation than would otherwise be the case, if you rather than I escort him around the Fordbridge site.'

'You think he resents dealing with you in your position, because of your sex?' Arnold asked in surprise.

She held his glance levelly, a hint of suppressed irritation in her eyes. 'Look, let's just leave it. Allow me to bring my instincts into play. I think it better that you show him Fordbridge . . . and hopefully give him no reason for making suggestions to the FCAI committee that might cause them to renege on their commitment.'

'You think they're likely to?' he asked, frowning.

She hesitated, watching him in careful assessment. 'I don't know . . . It's always possible. Mind you, I'm trusting you with this assignment, but it's not without hesitation, Arnold.'

'What's the problem?' he asked.

She picked up a pencil on her desk, played with it, twisting it between her slim fingers. He thought the colour of her eyes might be green . . . or possibly hazel. Colours seemed to change with her mood. 'The problem may be Dr Midgley.'

'Charles Midgley?' Arnold had a cold feeling in his chest. His mouth was suddenly dry. 'What about him?'

'I get the distinct impression he's not too happy with you,' Karen suggested, a hint of calculation in her tone.

Arnold was unable to keep the defensiveness out of his own voice. 'What . . . what makes you say that?'

'He's been on the phone. He told me that Martin Woudt was across here on business, and would be bringing details of the FCAI funding with him. It was Midgley who suggested it would be a good idea for him to be shown over the Fordbridge site. And then your name came up.'

'In what context?' Arnold asked, with a sinking feeling in his stomach.

Karen Stannard's tone was non-committal. 'Oh, we talked a bit about the conference, and he was kind enough to compliment me on my presentation. It was all very flattering, so I found it necessary to add that it was really a team effort, the investigation at Fordbridge, like the one at Abbey Head. I even sang your praises.' She smiled sweetly at him, with the mockery of a cat playing with a helpless mouse. 'Is that a surprise to you, Arnold?'

He ignored the comment. 'So where did the problem come in?'

She shrugged. 'His reaction was surprising. His tone was dismissive. And it became very clear to me that he doesn't like you, Arnold. I can't *imagine* why,' she purred. 'Have you done something to upset him?'

He shook his head, aware of the discomfort in his chest, unable to meet her glance directly. 'I can't think what I might have done to upset him,' he lied. 'As far as I'm concerned, the time I spent in his company in Carcassonne was . . . friendly enough.'

She knew he was feeling uncomfortable and she watched him with eyes that had darkened with suspicion. He could guess what she was thinking — considering whether to pursue the matter. In the event, she decided not to press it. She sighed. 'All right, I'll take your word for it, but I can assure you that as far as Charles Midgley is concerned you're not his flavour of the month. But then I suppose boys will be boys in their petty little macho wars. Just one word of warning, nevertheless.' She held his glance and her eyes were cold. 'Don't make any mistakes with Dr Woudt. Give him the treatment, handle him with kid gloves, with deference, hell, creep to him if you have to. I don't want to hear any complaints about you from him, as well as Midgley.' She widened her mouth, the smile was mockingly tender. 'Otherwise, have a nice time, won't you?'

He had left her office with a feeling of relief. He was very much aware of the reason why Charles Midgley was upset. He could still recall the cold anger in the forensic scientist's tones when he had phoned through to Arnold's room the morning after Arnold had left the document case outside Midgley's room.

'It was you who left that case at my door?'

'Yes. I'm afraid I picked it up by mistake.'

'What the hell made you think it belonged to me?' Midgley snapped, making no secret of his anger.

'I . . . I don't know. I looked inside. I just thought that maybe . . . with your forensic work . . .'

'For God's sake, Landon, that stuff was just bloody pornography! Child abuse! How could you possibly think—'

The man's breathing was rapid, he was clearly upset and annoyed. But there was something else in his tone, an edgy nervousness, an uncertainty that disturbed Arnold.

'Anyway, it doesn't belong to me . . . and I've disposed of the filthy rubbish!' The phone was banged down furiously, back into its cradle.

Arnold had not spoken to Midgley again at the conference. They had managed to avoid each other during the remaining sessions and social events. On the last afternoon, Arnold had considered seeking him out, to apologize for the mistake he had made. But on reflection, he changed his mind. It was best that sleeping dogs were allowed to lie undisturbed. But even so, he was left with the odd feeling that when Dr Charles Midgley had phoned Arnold in righteous anger, there had been an undercurrent of nervousness also, leading Arnold to suspect that maybe the forensic scientist had not been telling the entire truth.

* * *

In the early afternoon, Martin Woudt declared himself well satisfied with what he had seen at the Fordbridge site. He shook hands with Arnold: his fingers were cool, his grip slack. He announced that he would be reporting back favourably to the FCAI committee. 'I shall of course, be able to visit the site again over the next few weeks. I have business . . . it will bring me back to the north-east from time to time. I am particularly interested in following the work on the coral beads and spacers . . . all those tiny blue beads. I think they may have formed part of a tassel. We have something at the Rijksmuseum which is similar. I must look at its provenance again. The possibility of Continental links is exciting. Perhaps this lady in the grave, maybe she was an immigrant, Mr Landon? I will look up some references and materials . . .'

'That would be most helpful Dr Woudt. Now, I'll give you a lift back—'

'That will not be necessary.' Woudt replied. He explained that one of the staff at the dig was going back to Newcastle so he had accepted the offer of a lift from the young man in question. Arnold was relieved to see him march off with the young university researcher, a Carcassonne document case tucked under his arm. Woudt, at least, was making good use of the case he had received at the conference. Arnold no longer possessed one, having left the case he'd picked up outside Midgley's door. But now, with Woudt's transport catered for, it meant that Arnold was able to take the opportunity to leave Fordbridge and move on to the sea cave work at Abbey Head. After Woudt had gone, Arnold drove towards the coast as the skies lightened, the sun emerged and the distant sea sparkled beyond the headland road.

He left his car on the headland, near the ruins of the abbey building. He glanced across to the deep cleft that was named Hades Gate and thought back to the events that had occurred there. He had no desire to go to its lip, and look down to where one man had been thrown, and another had fallen to his death. He walked slowly down the track that had been driven to the beach, to allow the passage of earth-moving equipment. He noted that the sea wall had now been rebuilt and strengthened, to protect the entrance to the sea cave itself.

As he crossed the beach, he saw Portia Tyrrel emerging from the cave. She was wearing a denim jacket over a loose, flapping shirt, tight jeans that emphasized the line of her slim thighs, and heavy boots. Her dark hair was tousled and there were smudges of dirt on her cheeks. Normally she was very precise about her appearance. When she saw him she peeled off her gloves, waved and came forward to greet him. Her eyes were mocking.

'What a surprise! Amazing, all the intellectual muscle coming down here today!'

'Hello, Portia. How's the work going along?'

'Fine,' she enthused, pushing back a stray wisp of hair, 'even if we do get held up by all these important people coming along to rubberneck.'

'Who are you talking about?' Arnold asked.

She grinned. 'There's you, of course. And then earlier on we had Dr Mwate. You've only just missed him. Hey, where did you *find* that guy? That man is *gorgeous*! That laugh, and those muscles! I almost swooned in his company, like a real Victorian maiden.' She affected a mock American accent. 'I mean to say, what a hunk! he's suhwayve, daybownayer, and he's got *charayisma*!'

Arnold laughed. 'And he's well qualified too. I suppose he came down to take a look at the shamanic paintings on the walls?'

'That's it. We spent quite a while in there, in the dim light. It was shivery. And when I sort of stumbled as we were coming out, and he put his arm around me, to steady me. Brrr . . .' She shuddered deliciously. 'The muscles on the guy!'

'You were impressed,' Arnold suggested ironically.

'And some.' She cocked her head on one side, appraisingly. 'And were you impressed with Carcassonne?'

He could guess what was coming, tried to sidetrack the inference. 'The city was fantastic. So well restored, you could almost feel you were back in medieval times. It was an interesting enough conference, as conferences go. And we managed to impress the FCAI committee into giving us the financial support we need at Fordbridge.'

'While I was slaving away down here,' she sighed mockingly. 'But that's not quite what I meant. Did you . . . er . . . did you get the chance to cosy up to Karen?'

'It was a working weekend,' Arnold replied coolly.

'Ah, come on,' Portia teased. 'Don't tell me that the warm Mediterranean breezes from Narbonne didn't get you two sighing under the stars, holding hands, releasing a few tensions and—'

'You've got a vivid imagination,' Arnold interrupted, only too well aware that she was slicing for bone. 'I'll go and take a look in the cave, see how things are going on.'

'Don't be too long,' she warned. 'I'm just going to clean up a bit. We'll be finishing work shortly.'

He nodded, and left her. There were just two people remaining in the cave, staff from the department in the process of packing up for the day. He spoke briefly with them, looked into the deeper recesses of the sea cave, shivering slightly at the memory of the ancient violence that had been part of its history, and pored for a while over the shamanic drawings that would have drawn Julian Mwate's attention. He smiled again at Portia's description of the Zimbabwean. She had been as charmed, he suspected, as the two research students Mwate had escorted around Carcassonne. Or maybe she was just mocking Arnold. One could never be entirely sure with Portia Tyrrel. She could be enigmatic in her motivation.

When Arnold re-emerged from the cave Portia was ready to leave. 'You got your own car, I suppose?' she asked.

'Left it on the headland.'

'Up near Hades Gate . . .' She eyed him quizzically. 'Anything new going on out here I don't know about?'

'What do you mean?'

'You know. Any sort of follow-up to all the trouble we had here last year.'

'I don't understand.'

She took a deep breath, looked around her, tucking her shirt carefully into her jeans, and buttoning her denim jacket. 'Well, when I said that all the muscle seemed to be turning up today, I wasn't just talking about you and Dr Mwate. There was someone else prowling around. So I just wondered whether there had been any other developments.'

'Someone else?' Arnold frowned, puzzled. 'Such as . . .'

'Such as Detective Chief Inspector Culpeper. He was up on the headland, came down, stopped by for a chat.' Arnold shook his head. 'No longer DCI. He's retired.'

'I wouldn't know about that,' Portia shrugged indifferently. 'But he was wandering around here earlier.' She eyed him suggestively. 'Even invited me to join him for a drink, after I'd finished here. The Black Horse, up at Abbey village. Must have known I go for older men. Or any men.' She grinned. 'This time, I declined. I mean, even I draw the line at a corpulent, retired copper!'

After she had driven off, Arnold walked slowly back up the track to the headland, and the ruined abbey. He stood there for a little while on the short-cropped sward, gazing out to sea. The storm clouds had gone but on the horizon a shadow crept slowly across the blue, white-capped water. He wondered what Culpeper had been doing up here on the headland. He shivered slightly as he recalled the last time the man had been here. Death had been around them, had almost touched them. He went back to his car, started the engine, drove slowly along the track to the main road. It was almost without thinking that he took the side turning to Abbey village.

He caught sight of Culpeper's broad back as soon as he entered the lounge bar. Thick-waisted in his blue shirt, leather body-warmer and faded jeans, he still affected a short stubble cut for his grey hair. He had one booted foot on the bar rail and he turned to glance back at the newcomer to the bar. His wide mouth broke into a grin as he recognized Arnold. 'Well, well . . . I was half hoping it might be that young woman you got working down at the sea cave. But you'll do to pass the time with, Landon.'

'Retirement proving too slow for you?' Arnold asked.

'Wife says I get under her feet. After decades of my never being there, and even failing to turn up for holidays up at Seahouses, now she's got me there, even that isn't right. Drink?'

Arnold told him a lager would be acceptable. After Culpeper had ordered it from the barman Arnold looked around the room. 'I remember this place well enough.' Culpeper raised an eyebrow. 'Ah, yes, bonny lad, it was here you got involved in a fight with those local yobbos.' He chuckled. 'Wouldn't have minded being in on that.'

'As I seem to recall, you did get involved, up at Alnwick. But that was all a while ago. What brings you up here, and wandering around Abbey Head? I thought everything had been tied up, filed away in that investigation. And besides, you're retired.'

Culpeper paid for the drinks and gestured towards a table near the window. When they sat down he grimaced, bared his teeth and said, 'Well, you can guess how it is. Wife wants me out of the house, can't go fishing up at Seahouses by meself, so I just thought I'd indulge in a bit of nostalgia, wander around the scenes of my old triumphs. Been down to Shields one day, and Newcastle another; up in the Simonside Hills, and Berwick, across to Morpeth and Alnwick. Just tramping where all my life happened. Today, it was the turn of Abbey Head.'

'Interesting memories?' Arnold asked, sipping his drink.

'I can recall more than a few bruises,' Culpeper grumbled. 'Still, no complaints. It's just that retirement is . . . different.'

Carefully, Arnold said, 'From what I read in the newspapers, your retirement wasn't the only one.'

There was still some loyalty to the pack in Culpeper, irritation glinted momentarily in his eyes when he glanced at Arnold. Then he blinked, and shrugged. 'Aye, well, it happens I suppose. When you're top brass, temptations come your way. Not money so much, because there's plenty of that bein' shoved in your face when you're in the crime squad. No, power, and favours given, and rubbing shoulders with people who maybe made their money the wrong way, as well as with those with titles and political clout. Ah, hell, the Old Man and the ACC, they were guilty of stupid vanity, rather than anything criminal. But, the way of the world being as it is, they had to go.'

'At least you left untarnished,' Arnold said.

Culpeper's seamed old eyes regarded him for a little while, then he ducked his head in acknowledgement. 'In a job like mine was, no one ends up entirely without some muck sticking.' He considered the matter for a little while, then added, 'Maybe that's why this guy is calling in here to see me this afternoon.'

'You have a meeting?'

'My successor, no less.' Culpeper gave a sardonic grin. 'Fancy that. A DCI coming out here, just to see me! Must be important.'

'I'll get out of your way—'

'Naw, bonny lad, no need for it. I reckon it'll just be general stuff, and anyway, I'm a civilian now. I can choose who I want to spend time with. Besides, you owe me a drink, and with my pension I can't afford to be open-handed all the time.'

DCI O'Connor arrived at the pub some twenty minutes later. He stood uncertainly in the doorway, tall, slimly built, dark-haired with features that were hawkish, saturnine in cast. He glanced around, caught sight of the two men, hesitated, then walked across.

'Culpeper.'

'DCI O'Connor.'

'Jack will do,' O'Connor replied. He glanced at Arnold, looked him over, weighing him up with a cool glance.

'This is Arnold Landon,' Culpeper explained. 'I wouldn't say we're exactly old friends, but we've been through some . . . *situations* together. We was just having a drink for old times' sake. No reason why he shouldn't hang around while we have our little chat? Jack?'

Arnold would have preferred to leave, not least when he saw the uncertainty in O'Connor's eyes. But then it faded. Both he and Arnold knew what was going on. This was Culpeper showing he was no longer tied by the old constraints. He was an ex-copper, and he made up his own mind. He had no orders to follow now; he was his own master.

Arnold wondered also whether there was a certain resentment in Culpeper, as he looked at the younger man holding down the job he had undertaken for so long.

After O'Connor had bought a round of drinks and rejoined them at the table, Culpeper asked mischievously, 'So how's Farnsby?'

'Sore.' O'Connor held Culpeper's glance. 'And still moaning on about you.'

Culpeper guffawed. 'Hey, it's good to feel you've left an impression even after you've gone!' He puffed out his cheeks reflectively. 'But Farnsby, well, I rode him a bit, but he's not a bad lad at heart. And a pretty good copper.'

'You never told him so,' O'Connor suggested.

'Hey, what was I, a wet nurse? He got enough kudos from the Old Man. No one ever coddled me,' Culpeper grumbled.

'You wouldn't have wanted it.'

'No, well, maybe not. The streets were my education.' Culpeper sipped his drink, eyeing O'Connor over the rim of the glass. 'So what did you want to see me about?' O'Connor's glance side-slipped towards Arnold and he shrugged diffidently. 'Just talk over old times, I suppose.'

'Bollocks! You want something. Maybe I can help. An old fox like me . . . Can't be the Starlight Club investigation. It was ongoing when I left. I hear you got those child-abusing bastards under arrest.'

'All bar one.' O'Connor looked again at Arnold, as though wondering how far he could go. Then he shrugged. 'On the website he's called The Doctor. We haven't yet identified him. But it's not that.'

'So talk to me. And don't mind Landon here. He's discreet.'

O'Connor waved his glass dismissively. 'Nothing secret in what I want to chat about. It's just something Farnsby said to me . . . and the general chatter in the office. They all tell me you'd been *around* a long while.'

O'Connor wasn't talking about length of service, Arnold concluded. There was an underlying emphasis marking his tone. Culpeper caught it too. The retired policeman laughed. 'That's right enough, bonny lad. Back streets, cellars, wharves, quayside, alleyways, I been down them all in my day. Seen all the river rats, chased all the city foxes. It's down in those places, that's where you learn things. Not out of the books young Farnsby was nurtured on.'

O'Connor nodded. 'You sound like my old man.'

'Sensible guy, then. Copper, was he?'

O'Connor nodded. 'He made sergeant. Much your age. Not as fit as you now, though . . . retirement broke him.' O'Connor thrust away the thought in sudden irritation. 'The thing is, Culpeper, we've got a pretty big problem on our hands right now.' He glanced again at Arnold. 'You'll both have read enough about it in the newspapers. Along with the wild theories.'

Culpeper considered the matter slowly. 'Doesn't take much to make a guess. The torso, in the river.'

'That's right.' O'Connor took a stiff pull at his gin and tonic. 'You can appreciate what it's like. Nothing from forensics that's of much help. No dental records, no fingerprints, no missing person report—'

'And no obvious motive.' Culpeper's attitude had sharpened. He nodded in sympathy. 'It must be a bugger.'

There was a short, contemplative silence. As they sat there Arnold's thoughts drifted away from the present topic of conversation to something O'Connor had said earlier. The Starlight Club. He had read of it in the newspapers, and of the arrests. But now, DCI O'Connor had spoken of one man still undetected. A man they called The Doctor. Arnold thought about the contents of the document case he had found in the hotel in Carcassonne . . .

'Of course,' O'Connor was saying negligently, 'as you well know, we have to pursue every line of enquiry. Even the more outlandish. And there's one thing come up, which I find way out of the ballpark, so to speak, but it's been put forward seriously. So I have to consider it. And I just wondered whether, in your experience on Tyneside . . .'

'What you on about, Jack?' Culpeper asked, his eyes pouching in curiosity.

'Something called *muti*,' O'Connor replied.

Culpeper leaned back in his chair. 'What the hell's that?'

There was a short silence. 'You never heard of it?' O'Connor asked.

In spite of himself, the words came out from Arnold's lips. 'Traditional African medicine. Practised by *sangomas*. Witch doctors.'

O'Connor's head turned slowly. His eyes were cold, appraising. His tongue flicked over his lips. 'That's right,' he said quietly. His glance remained on Arnold, shaded by a barely veiled animosity.

'*Muti*,' Culpeper muttered. He shook his head. 'Can't say I've ever come across it. Not up here in the north-east. And I go back a long while.'

Almost casually, O'Connor asked, 'What about ritual killings?'

Culpeper frowned, took a thoughtful sip of his beer. 'Ritual . . . African . . . Now what do I recall . . . There was that Nigerian case back, what, twenty, thirty years ago? No, not Nigerian . . . where the hell did the family come from originally? There was some wild talk of a *sangoma* then, but it was all a bit silly . . .' He frowned. Abruptly, he snapped, 'It was a missing kid.'

O'Connor leaned forward. 'An abduction?'

Culpeper shook his head. 'Naw . . . it was all so long ago, and we never did find what exactly happened. The mother reported her boy missing . . .there was quite a noise about it for a while, and then . . . what happened? It all died down. But the family, they weren't Nigerians . . . where were they from, dammit? And anyway, in the end it was all just talk. You know, newspaper talk about witch doctors and ritual killings, black magic, all that sort of nonsense. The mother, in the end, she just withdrew, said the kid had gone back to Africa. Hey, we had plenty else on our plates, we weren't about to go chasing a case that wasn't there.' He picked up his glass, scraped it along the table in front of him. 'Not much help, really. Sorry about that.'

O'Connor shrugged. 'Was there a file on the case?'

'Should be. If the likes of young Farnsby haven't dumped it years ago. But most of it will be up here anyway,' Culpeper added, tapping his head. 'Real library here, you ask anyone back at Ponteland.'

O'Connor drained his glass. He sucked at his teeth despondently. 'Well, if you can dredge anything out of your

. . . library, I'd appreciate you letting me know.' His eyes turned to Arnold thoughtfully. 'You're an archaeologist, right?'

'Of a kind.'

'The practice of *muti* come into your field, then?' Arnold shook his head. 'Not really. It's just that I was having a conversation with someone last weekend. The topic came up . . .'

'Is that so?' O'Connor's eyes had darkened with an occupational suspicion. 'It just came up . . .'

'A university professor. At a conference in Carcassonne.' Arnold felt suddenly confused by the glitter in O'Connor's eyes. 'We were talking about it briefly. A Dr Julian Mwate.'

O'Connor's eyelids flared in surprise. He looked away, staring at his empty glass. Then he glanced at Culpeper. The retired detective had shifted in his chair, was frowning, leaning forward to glare at Arnold.

'Who . . . what did you say that name was?' Culpeper asked harshly. His tone was stained with suspicion.

CHAPTER THREE

1

Inspector Raoul Garcia was slimly built, dark-moustached, of middle height, and his swarthy skin was tanned. He clearly cared for the way he looked: his suit was immaculately cut, his pink designer shirt complemented by a matching tie, and his elegant Italian shoes were highly polished. His eyes were a deep, intelligent brown; his eyelashes almost feminine in their length. His hair was long and black, swept back smoothly, but there was a light dusting of grey at his temples, and the lines around his mouth were deeply cut, cicatrices of experience. He could be dogmatic, O'Connor knew, and arrogant, but he was also able to admit to his mistakes. O'Connor liked him.

They had worked together a year ago in the investigation into the death of a man picked up by a Spanish fishing boat and they had got on well together. Now, meeting again, Garcia extended his hand to take O'Connor's in a firm grip.

'Jack. Good to see you again, *amigo*.'

His English was accented, but accurate. O'Connor smiled and waved him to a chair. 'So you've come over to assist us in the African boy murder.'

'I jumped at the chance to work with you again,' Garcia replied with an expansive spreading of his hands. 'When I saw the information request come in, and realized it was from you, I thought it would be good to come back to the northeast for a while.' He smiled, a flash of white, even teeth below his dark moustache. 'I like your Newcastle pubs.'

O'Connor returned the smile. 'I'm sure we'll be able to fit in a few visits. But I presume you've come up with something, regarding our requests.'

Garcia nodded vigorously. 'We have. We ran your request through our database, and we managed to find a match for the tartan cloth that the boy was wearing. You already told us you had discovered it was distributed by a company in the UK called Kidwear.'

O'Connor nodded. 'Under licence.'

'Well, the owner of the design pattern is a German firm, based in Hamburg. And the bad news is that it looks as though the material itself was not in fact manufactured in the UK as you had assumed. The Hamburg company insist that the structure of the material itself tells them it was made by a separate company, also under licence, based in The Hague.'

'The Netherlands?' O'Connor clicked his tongue in annoyance. 'That means the boy could have come from Europe. That causes problems . . .'

'It means your search will widen,' Garcia agreed, with a sympathetic twist of the mouth. 'But at least it gives you a lead, you can look at immigration entries—'

'With the number of bloody illegals we've got pouring in through the Channel ports every year?' O'Connor scoffed. 'Get real my friend. Our ports are leaking like a sieve. It's not just the Channel Tunnel. Our controls at all the entry points on the south and east coasts — they're laughable. And apart from that, we just don't have a starting point. No reports of missing kids, no distraught relatives—'

'That's not the case in Europe,' Garcia interrupted quietly. 'We've had a regular list of such reports. I agree, identification is difficult because a large number of the people involved have come from families who have entered Europe illegally. There's a regular run from Ceuta and Morocco into

Spain where many stay, scraping out a living; from there the illegals spread out into Germany and Italy. You have a major problem in the UK with Afghans, Iraqis, Pakistanis. Elsewhere in Europe the problem is an African one. A large proportion consists of summer workers who come in to harvest the fruit crops — but many stay on illegally to swell the numbers of those entering to ensure for themselves a better economic future.'

O'Connor frowned. 'And you say you have reports of missing children?'

Garcia nodded. 'A considerable number. We're not sure, but we think they may have been sold into a form of slavery.'

'Sexual?'

'It is an option,' Garcia agreed carefully, shrugging an elegant shoulder. 'However, we are now checking whether we can find any match with your case, and any missing reports we hold. The trouble is, as you'll appreciate, the information you have is so thin. The illegals, they do not wish to advertise their presence. But, in respect of the torso, have you come up with any theories yet?'

O'Connor leaned back in his chair and folded his arms.

He shook his head doubtfully. 'We're looking at a couple of options. The obvious one is that the head and limbs were removed because identification was important. Knowing who the boy was could lead us to the killer. But there's another line of enquiry we're pursuing. The practice of *muti*.' He saw the puzzlement in Garcia's eyes, and added, 'There's a view been put to us that maybe someone in the north is in the business of taking body parts and using them for so-called medicinal purposes. We're looking at old files right now, seeing if there's any other instances we can pin down.'

'*Muti* . . .' Garcia's dark eyes were doubtful. 'Body parts . . . It sounds bizarre . . . I can hardly believe that such practices . . .'

'There are others who do believe it.'

'And you?'

O'Connor unfolded his arms, looked at the ceiling, raised the palms of his hands despondently. 'Hey, like I said, we don't even have a starting point. We have to look at all possibilities.'

Raoul Garcia was silent for a little while. His right hand stole up to his face; absent-mindedly he began to smooth his moustache. 'I was going to suggest to you that maybe there is another starting point, if we look at what's been happening in Europe in the last two years.'

O'Connor stared at him, his interest quickening. 'Talk to me.'

'This *muti* theory, I would not wish to discount it,' Garcia said carefully, 'though we at Interpol have no record of similar activities elsewhere in Europe. On the other hand, I personally have been working on a series of cases, which was one reason why I asked for this assignment. There may be a connection.'

'How do you mean?'

Garcia pursed his lips thoughtfully. 'Eighteen months ago, the naked torso of an eight-year-old white girl was found near a lake resort in an eastern province of the Netherlands. It was a horrible experience for the children who found the body. They had been swimming in the lake when they came across the object. An investigation commenced . . . but it was only some days later that the head was found. It was dredged out of a canal, some sixty miles distant from the lake. Near the entrance to the ferry terminal at the Hook of Holland. The terminal serves Harwich, in England.' His dark eyes flickered up to O'Connor, held his glance for a long moment.

'Was the child ever identified?' O'Connor asked harshly.

'I fear not.' Garcia sighed, despondently. 'Cases like these, they are . . . difficult to come to terms with. The Dutch police are demoralized. They have no leads, only problems similar to yours. We have been working with them, and we've also brought in a psychological profiler. He is working on the Netherlands case. And also there is the young student from Finland.'

O'Connor chewed at his lip thoughtfully. 'Similar circumstances?'

Garcia shrugged expressively. 'Fifteen-year-old girl. Caucasian. She was found in the Rhine. Feet removed, along with the hands. Facial tissues removed. We did find that there were high levels of mercury content in her remaining tissues, which excluded the possibility of her having lived in certain areas of the country. So we've managed to slim down the number of locations, where she might have come from. We've concluded her home was in Finland; precisely where, we're not yet sure.'

'But no identification?'

Garcia shook his head, his tanned forehead creased in a frown. 'Not yet. But as far as the killer is concerned, we are now developing, with the help of the psychological profiler, a certain theory.'

'Tell me.'

Garcia took a silver cigarette case from his jacket pocket, extracted a cigarette, held it between his fingers but made no attempt to light it. 'It's a logical assumption that when a killer removes head and limbs the purpose would be to prevent identification, from dental records and fingerprints. It was the initial theory. But then another was suggested to us — the purpose would be similarly served by removal of the hands and feet rather than entire limbs — which I am informed are more difficult to sever. The fact that the killer has chosen to do so would seem to suggest that the motive might have been to make the body more easy to transport.' He stared gloomily at the unlit cigarette. 'Not identification, but transport.'

'I see your point . . .' O'Connor's mouth twisted in doubt. 'One thing worries me though, if you're suggesting that our headless torso has a real connection with the cases you've mentioned you're working on. I'll agree that instances of dismembered children are unusual, and the discovery of three within . . . what . . . eighteen months . . . ?'

Garcia nodded, tapping the cigarette on its case. 'Thereabouts.'

'Well, I'll agree it starts alarm bells ringing. But I doubt if there's enough evidence to warrant combining the investigations. All right, two of the kids were of a similar age, each of them had been decapitated, and disposed of in water. On the other hand, there's a gender difference, different races are involved, and the bodies were found in different countries.'

Garcia's features were grave. 'This is true. It is why I think you should still pursue your *muti* enquiry. There may be no connection — merely coincidence. But I propose you also consider another possibility. That we have a serial killer on our hands, someone who works throughout Europe. Our profiler, Dr Erzin, he has given us a picture of the man we might be seeking. He will be a white man, probably married, in his late thirties perhaps. And he works in a job that allows him to travel throughout Europe.'

'Like a lorry driver?'

'Exactly. And if there is a connection with your African boy, we can now say that this man will have travelled regularly in the Netherlands, Germany, Finland . . . and Britain.'

O'Connor ran a hand over his face, as though brushing away cobwebs. Dismembered bodies of young children. There were times when the job he had to do disgusted him.

Garcia seemed to know what he was thinking. 'There is also satisfaction to be gained,' he said quietly, 'when these monsters are brought to account for their crimes.'

'Locked up in relative luxury in a mental health institution?' O'Connor sneered. 'Or serving a few years and then vanishing back into the community to start all over again?'

'Human rights,' Garcia shrugged non-committally. 'At least we do have some successes.' He glared unhappily at the unlit cigarette, and with considerable reluctance returned it to its case, and the case to his jacket pocket. 'But they can come hard.'

O'Connor guessed he was half-referring to giving up smoking. 'What about the other enquiry we referred to you?'

'The other case we were supplying information on: your Starlight Club? The arrests have been made, I understand.'

O'Connor nodded. 'I'm not actually dealing with that one. But I gather Interpol was very helpful. Half a million pornographic images of children worldwide on the Internet.'

'Have you thought there might be a link with the African boy?' Garcia queried.

'We've found none so far. At the moment, DS Robinson, who's running the enquiry, is concentrating on trying to find out the identity of the one guy missing, the one who actually organized the website. We don't have a name. They all used pseudonyms and we've had no identification problem with any of the men we actually have in custody. But the one outstanding — he's just referred to as The Doctor.' He shook his head dolefully. 'We're under pressure of course, to get an early result. But we're pretty stretched . . . And sticking to one enquiry, especially a nasty one like this African boy, can be wearing.' He paused, eyed Garcia thoughtfully. 'You busy this afternoon?'

'I have no particular plans, my friend.'

'Fancy a trip down the river, to the coast?'

* * *

DI Farnsby was hesitant at first. He had already agreed, reluctantly, to O'Connor coming along but was doubtful about another officer being present. When O'Connor pointed out, however, that it might put further pressure on the man they were to see, in view of the European dimensions of the investigation, Farnsby agreed. Albeit stiffly and with bad grace.

Farnsby drove. He relaxed somewhat as Garcia chatted, questioning, curious about the areas they were driving through, eager to learn about the north and its culture and history. As they crossed the Tyne, Farnsby told him about the building of the High Level Bridge and pointed out the recent additional crossing provided by the sparkling new Millennium Bridge, curving elegantly across to the Gateshead bank. When the Jarrow signpost came up, he told the Interpol man about the last public hanging, two centuries earlier, at Jarrow Slake, and about the Jarrow March. That led to a discussion of the decline of industry along the Tyne and in the north generally, the loss of mining and the effect on pit villages, the destruction of the shipbuilding industry, the new emphasis on tourism and entertainment and culture. 'You should see the scene on a Saturday night,' Farnsby added. 'Young people pouring out of the Metro stations for a night out in the city clubs . . . Acres of female flesh, even in a bitter east wind.'

'My own birthplace, Valencia, has also seen many such changes,' Garcia confided. 'But this case you are working on, Mr Farnsby. I understand from our friend here that it has a European dimension.'

Farnsby nodded. 'That's right. About two years ago we started an investigation into a traffic in stolen cars. There was a high incidence of car theft throughout the north-east: expensive cars being nicked, apparently to order. Our enquiries led us to an organization at South Shields. It was suspected that the stolen vehicles were being done over, then shipped into Europe by way of the ferries from Hull, into Zeebrugge or Rotterdam. From there, the cars were driven into Spain and Germany. We guess the eventual destinations were African countries through Ceuta, and eastern Europe through Prague.'

'That would involve an international network of some dimension,' Garcia suggested as he looked out of the window to pick up glimpses of the Tyne.

'Big business,' Farnsby agreed. 'The South Shields operation would only be a small cog, one of many supplying the international distributors. It's the kind of scam a local guy would give his eye teeth to get into. We had our target. And that's where things got a bit unstuck, according to the files. It looked as though we could finger the source, here on Tyneside and in Northumberland and Durham, but the link into a European-based organization was more difficult. It was intended to deal with Interpol—'

'I never heard of an approach,' Garcia said, frowning, absent-mindedly taking out his cigarette case.

Farnsby grimaced, glanced briefly at O'Connor seated beside him. 'The investigation was closed down. There was a raid on a garage in South Shields, but there was nothing we could proceed with, no real evidence, and the enquiry was put into mothballs.'

'Just like that?' Garcia asked, his dark eyes puzzled.

'They said it was on grounds of cost. And priorities.' Farnsby hesitated. 'Anyway, it's now reopened.'

'Why now?'

Farnsby licked his lips. He checked for traffic at the junction and swung the car into the heavy traffic on the main road, leading towards the coast and South Shields. 'Would have been easier going by the Metro,' he muttered to himself. 'Right . . . Why now? Because we have a new chief constable and a new assistant chief. And the latter, Mr Cathery, has an old score to settle. With the man we're going to see — and maybe ruffle up a bit.'

Garcia smiled, and nodded. 'Power and revenge make interesting bedfellows.'

* * *

The plate glass windows of the car showroom glittered in the late afternoon sunlight. The car park to one side of the showroom was busy. Inside the showroom itself there were several people wandering about, inspecting the vehicles on display, running their hands over gleaming bodywork, admiring elegant leather upholstery, being advised on performance and torque and price. It was a top of the range display and the prices were not low. Garcia had lapsed, with a lit cigarette between his fingers he whistled between his teeth as he wandered off, checking out the Toyotas and Mercedes and the BMWs. O'Connor inspected the Jaguars and Porsches on display. Farnsby stood just inside the sliding doors to the showroom and waited until an eager, bespectacled, dark-suited young man bustled forward. 'Is there anything here that particularly attracts you, sir?'

Farnsby smiled thinly. 'I'm not here to buy. Just to chat.'

The eyes behind the spectacles blinked uncertainly. 'I'm sorry, sir, I don't understand—'

'Don Catford available?' Farnsby asked casually.

The smile was deprecating and knowing. 'Ah, Mr Catford doesn't actually attend to showroom business, sir.'

'This isn't showroom business. I told you, I'm not a buyer.' A well-dressed, middle-aged couple wandered past and Farnsby raised his voice. 'My colleagues and I would like to have a word with Mr Catford.'

'Colleagues?' The young man glanced around the showroom, flustered. 'May I enquire about your business, why you might wish to see Mr Catford?'

'We're coppers,' Farnsby announced loudly. The heads of the middle-aged couple turned.

The cheerfulness of Farnsby's tone did nothing to alleviate the young salesman's anxiety. The loudness of the announcement induced near panic as he looked wildly around to see if any other prospective customers had heard. He raised a nervous hand. 'Just one moment, I'll go and see whether Mr Catford is available.'

'I'm certain he will be,' Farnsby assured the salesman as he retreated towards the far doorway.

A few minutes later, as O'Connor and Garcia made their way back towards the doorway to rejoin Farnsby, the bespectacled salesman reappeared. He swallowed nervously. 'Mr Catford will see you in his office, gentlemen.'

Politely, Garcia stubbed out his half-smoked cigarette in an ashtray on the salesman's desk.

Don Catford's office was furnished with a degree of opulence. The leather chairs were expensive, finely tooled; the carpet was thick, the wallpaper was heavily patterned, the desk was wide, gleaming, polished oak, and the man behind it was dressed in an expensive suit of an Italian cut.

'Business looks good,' Farnsby suggested as he sauntered forward, O'Connor just behind him. Garcia closed the door behind them with a studied care.

The man behind the desk glowered. 'It won't stay that way if you guys come in scaring the shit out of my salesmen. Even if you think it'll need three to do it.'

Don Catford was in his late forties. There was something shiny and unreal about his features, as though he had been made up for a photographic session. His skin was scaly, his lips barely seemed to move when he spoke, and his taut jawline seemed unnaturally youthful as though he had submitted to the scalpel on more than one occasion. But if his features lacked movement and expression, his eyes did not: they were basilisk cold, something moving sluggishly in their depths as he contemplated the three men in front of him. His voice had a harsh edge. 'I'd ask you to sit down, if I thought you'd be staying.'

'Oh, we'll stay long enough for our purposes,' Farnsby said brightly. 'It's just an introductory visit really, so we can get to know each other.' He glanced around the office. 'Smart . . . New premises, it would seem. New address, new showroom. Like I said, business must be good.'

'It's been better,' Catford muttered. 'And a change of address was necessary, after the last visit from you bastards.'

'Before my time,' Farnsby announced breezily. 'Tell me about it.'

Catford's eyes glittered as his glance slipped from one man to another, as though summing each up for future reference. 'You'll have it on file. You came down on my garage and showroom up in Wilson Street and you turned the whole place upside down. You had a warrant to search and you did it thoroughly. You went through all my records, turned my computer files inside out, and what did you find? Bugger all.' He laughed discordantly. 'You wasted my time as well as your own, but you caused me a lot of trouble. Word spreads, in Shields like anywhere else. After the mess you made of my premises and my reputation I had to move.'

'But not very far,' Farnsby suggested amiably. 'And still not too far from Hull, and the ferries.'

Catford's eyes became lidded as he contemplated his hands. 'What's that supposed to mean?' he asked in a quiet, dangerous voice.

'It means we haven't forgotten the reason why we turned you over the first time. Too many stolen cars making their way into Europe, too many suspicions about your rate of growth, too many strange people visiting your premises. Knew most of the villains on Tyneside, did you? Particularly the ones who were into nicking cars?'

'I don't know what you're on about,' Catford replied sullenly.

'Aw, come on, Catford! We know you had a business going; you employed young tearaways to nick cars to the specifications you wanted. You doctored those cars before shipping them through Hull, into Europe. And I've no doubt you're still bloody well doing it!'

'You didn't prove anything last time,' Catford sneered. 'And you're on the wrong track now.'

'We might have proved it,' Farnsby said coldly. 'But you talked to a few people, didn't you? Your contacts. And they sorted it for you. A word here and there. A promise, a favour called in. We all know how it's done. Trouble is, they're all gone now, your friends. And you're in trouble, my bucko.'

Malice and suspicion moved in Catford's eyes, and there was a hint of uncertainty in his trap-like mouth. He shook his head. 'This is all just mouthing off. You got nothing on me. I'm a respectable, legitimate businessman—'

'Come off it,' Farnsby laughed mirthlessly. He looked back to O'Connor and Garcia, standing silently behind him. 'But I've been remiss. I haven't introduced myself, nor my colleagues here. I'm DI Farnsby. This is DCI O'Connor, and Inspector Garcia. He's from Interpol . . .'

Catford straightened slightly in his chair. He looked Garcia up and down, in studied contempt. His mouth was like iron, but his tongue flickered nervously against his lips.

'I haven't really filled them in on you, the respectable, legitimate businessman,' Farnsby continued scornfully. 'You're what now — late forties? And you've been a busy little man ever since you were fifteen! What rackets haven't you had a finger in? I'm told there was prostitution in Bristol.

Didn't you have a suspected involvement with that counterfeiting ring in Bath? Then there was the property scam in Manchester — that solicitor got twenty years, didn't he? Like the social worker who got a ten-year stretch for procuring girls for that nightclub circuit in Liverpool. You weren't involved in that, of course. Any more than you had a finger in the Cheshire burglaries — the gang who got pulled in kept their traps shut, yes? Hey, I could go on, but the list is too long. But don't start trying to persuade me that you're *legitimate*. Quick on your feet, yes. Able to jump out of something just before the door closes. But you've got a shady history, Catford, and leopards don't change their spots. You're in business, yes, but the dirtier it is, the more you seem to like it. Cars . . . oh yes, we're looking at that again. But I also wonder what else you've got your mucky fat fingers into since you arrived in the north!'

Catford's features were expressionless, but his eyes were hot with barely suppressed anger. 'I know what this is. I know why you're here. It's a roustabout, isn't it? And I can guess who's behind it. It's that bastard Cathery, isn't it?'

Farnsby smiled mockingly. 'Oh, you know our Assistant Chief Constable, do you? So you still do have contacts in high places.'

Catford struggled with himself, containing his anger with difficulty. 'This is harassment, this is. You've got nothing on me. You're just out to destroy my business. These wild accusations, these innuendoes, I know where they come from. Sid Cathery tried to fit me up years ago, and now we're on the same patch he's trying to do it again.' Catford's eyes glittered with malice. 'Well, you can tell him from me it ain't going to work. He ran me out once, closed me down, and it cost him when I took him on. But I had to move, my reputation was shot, and he was still on my back.'

He stood up, his face reddening as he stared at the men facing him. He was a big man, running to fat now, but still menacing. 'You can tell Cathery that I'm not backing down this time. I took him to court once, and I'll do it again if this harassment continues. And the next time, there'll be no out-of-court settlement, no saving of faces. If I have to, if he keeps pushing me, I'll go for Cathery's guts!' He took a deep, steadying breath, his jaw jutting fiercely at them. He clenched his fists, struggling to control himself. He took a deep, shuddering breath.

'I think, gentlemen,' he said in a cold tone, 'this interview is over. You can get the hell off my premises.'

Outside in the street, Garcia said, rolling expressive eyes, 'That is a man who is seriously pissed off.'

O'Connor laughed. 'Palatic with fury.'

'I do not understand your English.'

Farnsby did. And was satisfied.

2

When the news broke that the FCAI were to join with the Department of Museums and Antiquities in the further excavation of the Fordbridge site a press conference was called and reporters arrived from several of the nationals, in addition to the feature writers from the local newspapers. The conference was held in a local hotel in Morpeth and both Dr Mwate from the university and Dr Charles Midgley from the Gosforth forensic science laboratories were introduced to the gathering by Karen Stannard.

Joe Holderness turned up also. He sat at the back of the room beside Arnold, listening intently to the presentation. As questions were fired at the three fronting the conference he seemed somewhat uncomfortable. He turned his craggy face towards Arnold and scowled uncertainly. 'I didn't realize the dig was going to raise such interest,' he said, leaning forward with his patched elbows on his knees. 'And to a businessman like me, time is money. You know how it is . . . things are difficult. But maybe, well maybe you can sort of lose sight of the big picture.'

Arnold nodded, aware of the reluctant indecision in the builder's tone. 'I quite understand. The FCAI support will help us, though. We are going to be pushed to finish against your deadline, of course, but . . .'

'Aye, well,' Holderness shifted in his seat uncomfortably, 'maybe I was being a bit . . . hasty when I gave you that deadline. And things never go entirely to plan in the building industry anyway. Materials, contracts, schedules . . . we've had a few hold-ups of our own along the line, and . . .' His wary eyes flickered over the gathering of reporters. 'This is going to get pretty big coverage, you reckon?'

'Bigger than we had anticipated,' Arnold agreed. 'But it is an important site.'

Holderness lowered his head, considering. 'Of course, the FCAI will be getting some publicity out of this, their first support in the UK, I hear.'

'That's right.'

Holderness sighed. 'There'll be hoardings going up with their name on, as well as reports in the nationals . . . You know, Mr Landon, maybe I was a bit too hasty, last time we met.' His glance shifted to Arnold, flickered around the room again. 'Maybe I could hold off for a bit longer.'

Arnold smiled. 'That would be good, Mr Holderness. Of course, if it would help we could make mention of that today, and I could ensure that any public hoarding displays would have the name of your firm alongside our department and the FCAI, to show how co-operative and public-spirited you've been . . .'

The Yorkshireman looked at him with shrewd eyes. They understood each other. 'Aye. I think that would be most satisfactory.'

Arnold took a pen out of his pocket, tore a sheet from one of the pads that had been placed on the tables and made his way towards the front of the room. Karen Stannard watched him come. She frowned, concerned that he might be trying to upstage her. Old suspicions faded only slowly. He passed her the note, Dr Mwate turned his head and smiled at Arnold. Charles Midgley was answering a question, but he faltered as he caught sight of Arnold out of the corner of his eye.

Arnold returned to the back of the room. 'Aye, well, that'll be all right then,' Holderness muttered. 'I'll be away out of here. I wouldn't want to be embarrassed by a public thank you.'

Arnold grinned. He looked back to the stage. Karen had read the note, she looked up and nodded to him in satisfaction. When Midgley had finished answering the question put to him, Karen Stannard intervened. 'One thing we have perhaps not made entirely clear, is the fact that the speed and continued success of our excavations have been due in no small part to the cooperation we have received from a local firm, Holderness Builders, who own the site . . .'

She'd picked up the point quickly enough, Arnold conceded, as Holderness slipped out of the back of the room. While she spoke he glanced at the two men flanking her on the platform. Dr Mwate lounged in his chair, big, confident, smiling. From what he had gathered during the discussion with Culpeper and O'Connor, Arnold realized that the professor was now acting as a consultant to the local police in the matter of the headless torso found in the Tyne. But his mind kept slipping back to the expression on Culpeper's face when he had heard Mwate's name mentioned. He had said nothing of significance, but the name had clearly troubled him, and he had fallen silent for a while, digging back into his memory. Arnold had excused himself shortly afterwards, and left the two men together, aware that O'Connor was not entirely at ease in his presence, and perhaps feeling constrained in his discussions with Culpeper. It was only the dogged insistence of the retired DCI that had kept Arnold there, longer than he himself would have wished.

And then there was Charles Midgley. The pathologist had caught Arnold's glance once only, and had quickly looked away. It was obvious he still bore a grudge against Arnold for the mistake he had made in the hotel at Carcassonne.

Karen was winding up proceedings. The conference was breaking up. As the reporters left Karen raised a hand to

Arnold, calling him forward. 'Perhaps you'd like to join us for a drink in the lounge?'

She led the way into the hotel bar, Mwate and Midgley side by side, Arnold a little way behind. Arnold ordered the drinks as Karen seated herself in a patterned armchair, the two men shared a settee. When Arnold came back with a tray of drinks, Karen looked up. 'We've just been talking about Dr Woudt.'

'Yes?'

'It seems he may not be able to spend as much time on the project at Fordbridge as he was intending.'

'Problems at the Rijksmuseum?' Arnold asked.

Charles Midgley avoided Arnold's eye as he spoke. 'Not that so much. Problems with Martin himself. He's not a well man, you know. I think he's been finding his job at the museum somewhat stressful. He's tendered his resignation. He'll be leaving at the end of next week.'

'That's a surprise, and rather sudden,' Arnold replied, handing out the drinks. There had been a false note in Midgley's voice, a defensiveness that puzzled Arnold. 'Dr Woudt said nothing about it when he was up at Fordbridge with me. Indeed, he intimated that he'd be looking forward to spending time on the project, since business called him fairly regularly to the north-east.'

Midgley shrugged. Karen Stannard leaned forward, concern in her voice. 'What exactly is the problem with his health?'

'Heart murmur or something,' Midgley muttered abruptly. 'Anyway, he's going. And his departure from the Rijksmuseum means he'll be giving up his work with FCAI as well.'

'That will be a loss,' Mwate murmured. 'I found him knowledgeable. And incisive in his judgements.'

'That's as may be.' Midgley picked up his drink, and sipped at it, frowning. He seemed reluctant to pursue the matter. 'Anyway, there'll be a vacancy at the Rijksmuseum in due course. They'll be advertising immediately. And then there's the FCAI committee . . .' He was silent for a little while, thoughtful. 'I was discussing the matter on the telephone last night with James Stead. One of the comments that have been made by the Holborn Trust from time to time is that it's been noted we have no women on the committee. James thinks it's maybe time we changed that.' His glance flickered up to Karen. 'There would be various formalities to go through of course, but James and I, we wondered whether you would be interested in filling the vacancy, Karen.'

'Me?' Her surprise was genuine.

'It's the first I've heard of the suggestion,' Julian Mwate intervened enthusiastically, 'but I think it would be a splendid idea.'

'Clearly, it would be contingent upon you being able to spare time from your department to undertake committee work with us,' Midgley commented.

Karen Stannard glowed. She looked at Arnold, a glint of excited triumph in her eyes. 'Oh, I'm sure arrangements could be made . . .'

Arnold was certain of it. Karen Stannard had never allowed what she saw as minor problems to impede the march of her ambitions.

When Midgley announced he'd have to get back to the laboratory at Gosforth Mwate rose to his feet but Karen intervened, placing a slim, elegant hand on the Zimbabwean's arm. 'No, please, Julian. I know you brought Charles out to the press conference but allow me to take him to Gosforth. It will give me a chance to talk over the implications of FCAI membership with him. I'll have to talk to my own Chief Executive, Mr Powell Frinton, of course, but before that I need to discover exactly what will be involved in FCAI work. Arnold, there's no need for you to rush back. Stay on here for a while with Dr Mwate.'

After she had ushered Midgley from the room, Julian Mwate grinned at Arnold. 'She must be a delight to work with.'

'You could say that,' Arnold replied non-committally. 'Another drink?'

'Mineral water will do. Africans do not handle liquor well.'

'Even African Geordies?' Arnold teased. 'Weren't you brought up properly in the local culture?'

Mwate laughed. 'I was quite young when I returned to Zimbabwe with my family. Didn't have time to pick up the booze, fags and fish and chips culture.'

When he returned with the drinks Arnold sat down opposite the university professor. 'Why did you go back to Africa so soon? Did your family ever face racial problems when you lived in Fenham? I hope I don't offend you by asking.'

Mwate waved a huge, dismissive hand. 'Not at all. No, my recollection is that we were accepted readily into the community. My father and his brother, they worked on the railways. They were accepted. It was just that my mother never really settled . . . family problems, I suppose. And there were not many black faces around at that time of course — except those coming out of the pits, and that was a different matter,' he added, grinning widely.

'This was what . . . twenty-five years ago?'

'All of that,' Mwate murmured.

Arnold hesitated. 'It's just that I was talking to a retired policeman recently. Culpeper?'

Mwate frowned, shook his head. 'Can't say I've ever heard of him.'

'The practice of *muti* came up.'

'Really?'

There was a short silence. Mwate took a careful sip of his mineral water. 'It seems everyone wants to know about *muti* these days.'

'I gather you've been taken on by the police as a consultant.'

'News travels fast.'

'Oh, it was gossip really, and it just came up,' Arnold said dismissively. 'And you and I had spoken briefly about it, in Carcassonne. But then Culpeper mentioned a Nigerian family who lived in Newcastle a couple of decades ago. Something about a missing child. There was a certain amount of noisy speculation in the newspapers, it seems. Almost inevitably, they raised the question of ritual killings for some reason.'

Mwate grunted. 'Newspapers will also go for outlandish theories. It assists in sales.'

Arnold leaned back in his chair, eyeing Mwate quizzically. 'You say there weren't many African families in the area at that time. Did you ever come across the people involved in that business?'

Slowly and deliberately Julian Mwate shook his head. 'I have no recollection of having any contact with a Nigerian family in Fenham in those days. But you must remember, I was quite young. And for that matter, it might well have happened after I had returned to Zimbabwe with my family.' A pulse beat steadily in the vein in his forehead. 'This suggestion of Midgley's, about Karen joining the FCAI committee. You think she'll be able to take it on?'

Arnold smiled. 'I've no doubt about it. I think she'll be able to persuade Powell Frinton. To be fair to him, though he's a bit of a stuffed shirt, he's actually quite supportive of the idea of staff being involved in outside, prestigious activities.'

'More work will then devolve upon you?' Mwate asked.

'More than likely. But there is her assistant also.'

'Ha. The delectable Miss Tyrrel. Yes, I've met her, up at Abbey Head.' His eyes twinkled, and he winked at Arnold. Then he paused, and asked gently, 'What is the problem between you and Charles Midgley?'

'Is there one?' Arnold prevaricated.

Mwate recognized an evasion when he saw one. He chuckled deep in his chest. 'I'm pretty certain there is. I know Charles quite well. He is surprisingly dismissive when he speaks of you, in spite of the acknowledged reputation you have achieved in the archaeological field. That is unlike Charles. It cannot be envy . . . But then, he seems . . . different recently. It's almost as though he's under some kind of pressure, since the conference at Carcassonne.'

'The police work he's involved in?'

'I doubt that,' Mwate frowned. 'He's always been on top of his job in that context.'

'I can't imagine what else it might be,' Arnold lied. But then, he was not alone in prevarication.

When he had asked about newspaper coverage of a missing child twenty-five years ago Mwate had denied having any recollection of it. Yet Arnold was left with the distinct impression that Mwate had been dissembling, and had quickly changed the subject.

And then there was ex-DCI Culpeper. In the pub, as he had struggled to remember those days, he had not even been sure the African family concerned had been Nigerian.

Arnold now wondered whether they might have been from Zimbabwe.

3

Jeannette Bartoli was perhaps thirty-five years of age but her best years were behind her. She had a full, voluptuous figure, heavy-breasted and broad-hipped, but there were signs of loss of weight control. Her hair was dark and long, falling to her shoulders. Her eyes were black and bold and challenging, though pouched with experience. She was the kind of woman who would be enthusiastic in bed, O'Connor suspected, and would have had a love life that had started early. She would be noisy and open-hearted, and quick to take offence. He wondered about her name and origins. Italian parentage, probably, quick-tempered, passionate. But now, with her bruises, sullen.

O'Connor had been in his office reading the forensic reports yet again, seeking some lead to pick up, when the young uniformed constable had tapped on the door, opened it and looked in a little nervously. His fresh cheeks were red with self-importance, his breathing quick.

'Yes?' O'Connor snapped, irritated at his own frustration as much as the interruption.

'Uhh, could I have a word, sir?'

'About what?'

The fresh-faced constable swallowed. 'It's a bit . . . well, fact is, sir, we was called out last night to deal with a domestic. This guy, beating up his partner.' He pushed out his chest, self-importantly. 'The pair of them, they weren't about to calm down so we had to haul them in, especially when she gave a right-hander to one of the constables.'

'Do I need to hear this?' O'Connor growled impatiently.

The young man shifted uneasily on his feet. 'I wouldn't bother you, sir, if I didn't think it important,' he replied somewhat indignantly, losing a little of his deference. 'But she's been screamin' all morning about her partner having killed someone. I just thought at first it was hysteria, all part of the domestic, you know how it is, wantin' to get at her old man, but now I'm not so sure.'

'Constable, we're up to our necks already in work. If this is a domestic, can't you handle it without reference to me?'

'Yes, but she's been saying some other things, as well.' What he had then outlined had drawn O'Connor down to the police cells.

The woman stared at him with hot, angry, distrustful eyes. He noted the swelling bruise on her cheek, the finger-marks on her throat, the scratches on her breast where her blouse had been torn away. She had made little attempt to draw it together. Her breasts were well used to male attention. 'So,' O'Connor said gently, advancing into the room and leaning against the wall with his arms folded. 'What's been going on?'

'Who the hell are you?'

'DCI O'Connor,' he replied calmly. 'And you're Jeannette Bartoli. Making wild accusations, I'm informed.'

'Not so wild,' she flared angrily. 'It's the truth! It's that mad, jealous bastard. Tried to kill me last night.'

'You'd better tell me all about it.' O'Connor suggested, raising his eyebrows at the woman police officer seated beside the indignant prisoner.

'I got to go over it again?' she complained. 'I already told the others. They got to lock George up and throw away the bloody key. He's homicidal. He goes nuts. Can't get things out of his head. And I haven't seen Saul for a week, and I know that George has done him in. Saul wouldn't just up and leave, not without telling me!' Her voice had risen to a wail, and she was close to tears, her pouched eyes red-rimmed.

O'Connor held up an admonitory hand. 'You'd better start at the beginning,' he suggested soothingly. 'Then maybe we can sort things out.'

Her fingers crept up to gently touch the bruises on her jaw and cheek, then caressed the redness at the top of her breast where fingernails had scored their tracks. 'That mad bastard,' she muttered. 'George, he's always had a violent temper.'

'And you'd upset him?'

'Well, he's away a lot, you know? And things get quiet around the place—'

'What place?'

'We rent a terrace house, down in Benwell. Victoria Street.'

'And things get quiet there.'

She nodded, her dark hair falling over her face. 'Yeah, and with George being away so much what am I supposed to do? Sit in that bloody back kitchen and twiddle my thumbs every evening? So what if I went out down the boozer a few times with Saul—'

'Saul?'

'He collects the rent for the landlord,' she said defiantly. 'Calls once a week. We got to chatting. He's a nice guy. Younger than George, and he knows how to please a woman, you know? So what the hell was wrong with going out for a bit of fun when George was off God knows where? There was no harm in it. Saul was just company. A bit of a laugh.'

She fell silent. O'Connor waited, then suggested, 'George didn't quite see it that way?'

'There was no need for him to know anything about it, and I tell you, it was all innocent anyway. All right, a bit of cuddling, when he brought me back to the house and I'd had a few drinks, but the bloody nosy neighbours . . . It was all the fault of that old harridan Mrs Jenkins, she stuck her nose in, told George I had a fancy man. George had a go at me about it and there was a hell of a row.'

'Last night?'

She grimaced contemptuously, and shook her head, her dark hair falling across her face. She pushed it back with an impatient hand. 'Naw, man, this was weeks ago! Then it all settled down for a while, but I could see George was suspicious and I did my best to make it up with him but the mad bastard, he kept niggling on at me. That got me mad too, like he didn't trust me. Maybe that's why I went out with Saul again, when George was away. But the cunning bugger come back unexpected, didn't he? And he caught us. All right, we was in bed, but that was no reason for him to act so crazy. He dragged Saul out and thumped him, threw him out into the street, no trousers on. But that wasn't enough. He kept brooding on about it, and then one day we had a few words again, and one thing led to another and George, he went out and I didn't see him all the rest of the day. And when he came back, I knew he'd been around to Saul's. Gave him a real good thumping this time, he told me.' She glared at O'Connor as though he was in some way responsible for the whole situation. 'But I know now it wasn't just a thumping. He killed him. He bloody well killed him!'

Patiently, O'Connor asked, 'And what makes you believe that?'

'Well, Saul's not been in touch, has he? I've been around to his house and it's all locked up. I left notes. But there's been nothing. I know in my guts what's happened! He went around there, the mad, crazy bastard, and he beat Saul up so bad that he killed him. Then he stuck him in the back of the lorry and he took him off somewhere, buried him. I just know it! You got to jail that madman, stick him away where he can't do no more damage. And you got to find what happened to Saul!'

O'Connor scratched at his jaw thoughtfully. 'You had a fight last night.'

'That's right,' she agreed dully, breathing hard after her outburst. 'He'd been drinking, and when he got home I asked him about Saul and he got mad, thumped me, and I went for him and it ended up with the neighbours calling the polis. That copper, he got up my nose. He wouldn't listen, kept telling me to calm down, didn't seem to understand what the hell's been going on. He took my arm, and that's an assault, right? I know my law! So I took a swing at him, self-defence like. And we both ended up on the floor, and then George lost his rag. That bloody Mrs Jenkins, she was on the doorstep when they shoved us into the squad car and brought us down here. The old hag,' she muttered bitterly, 'she and the others, they'll all be gossiping up and down the bloody street by now. Telling everyone I'm a slag.' She looked up in angry defiance, glared at O'Connor. 'But at least I don't go around killing people.'

O'Connor shrugged. 'We've sent a car around to Saul Bovey's place. We'll be looking into the matter. And we've got George in the cells. But you need to cool down, calm yourself. Stop making wild accusations.'

'But I know he's killed Saul,' she insisted, tears starting to well in her red-rimmed eyes. 'You got to find him. He said he'd get me away . . .'

'We'll find him, I'm sure,' O'Connor soothed. 'But when I said wild accusations, I wasn't just talking about Saul Bovey. I understand you've been saying other things too.'

She stiffened. Her glance dropped from his, she brushed the back of her hand over her eyes and lowered her head. 'I say lots of things when I'm upset.'

'And you're not upset now?'

She was silent. He knew what was happening. Cooperation with police enquiries was anathema to some people. It was one thing to bring her troubles with her partner to the police, it was another to co-operate, help them with anything else. He wondered whether, when it came to it, she would even press charges against George. Though the fact that Saul Bovey was missing, and she was obviously deeply involved with him, if only as an escape route from a difficult relationship, meant that she probably would go through with her complaints.

'We can help find Saul,' he prompted her, 'if you give us all the information you've got. You say George has killed him. Now if we had some corroborative information, maybe if you could show us his violence extended to that sort of action . . .'

She was not rising to the bait. O'Connor shouldered himself from the wall, and headed for the door. She looked up. 'So what are you going to do now?'

He glanced back over his shoulder. 'Nothing. This is just a domestic. We've no evidence that Saul Bovey's been killed. If he got a second beating from George, maybe he had the sense to get the hell out of Tyneside.'

'So what's going to happen?' she asked querulously. 'Come on, Jeannette, you know the score! You swear a complaint. We hold George, give him a talking to, take him before the magistrates. He gets charged with assault, obstructing the police or whatever, and then he'll get bail until the hearing—'

'You can't do that!' she wailed. She rubbed the heel of her hand against her nostrils. 'Haven't you been listening? George, he'll bloody well kill me when he gets out!'

'Our hands are tied,' O'Connor shrugged indifferently. 'We've nothing more serious to hold him on.' He stared at her, his eyes hard. 'Unless you've got something more to tell us. Something maybe you hinted at earlier on, when you were talking to the constable . . .'

She struggled with it. She sniffed noisily, her eyes wet with tears. Her instincts told her to keep her mouth shut, but fear scored her mouth, glittered through the moisture in her eyes. She shook her head. 'He was just talkin', when he was mad, like. It was just talk . . .' Then she thought of Saul Bovey, and her tone became grim. 'But that mad bastard, he's capable of anything . . . I don't know.' She looked up, her voice scored with fear and doubt. 'Thing is, when he was mad last night, he said something about . . .'

'Yes?' O'Connor prompted.

'He said something about that African kid. You know, the one they found without any head . . .'

* * *

123

George Baggs was a big man, perhaps forty years of age, broad-shouldered, a bit paunchy, but clearly still able to punch his weight. His brown hair was cut aggressively short; his nose was bent to one side, a bad setting of an old break. His mouth was discontented and his shaggy eyebrows were knitted together in a frown. He sat slumped in his chair in the interview room, sullen, resistant, but his fingers twitched nervously, and he kept his head lowered, unwilling to meet their eyes.

Raoul Garcia had asked if he could sit in on the interview when he had heard about the arrest, and what Jeannette Bartoli had said. O'Connor had agreed, he had a respect for the Interpol man, and it could help speed things along if they came up with what they were hoping to hear.

O'Connor opened the file on the desk in front of him. Farnsby had been right: Culpeper had always filed away information that might be useful at some time in the future, and they'd managed to come up with a history of George Baggs that went way back. 'Well then, George, you been around a bit, haven't you?'

George Baggs made no attempt to lift his heavy head. His hands were linked between his knees and he sat there, stolidly, unmoving.

'What do we have here . . . ? At fifteen you were earning a few quid in a boxing booth at the Hoppings.' When Garcia turned his head in query, O'Connor explained, 'Big fair on Newcastle Town Moor. Goes back a hell of a time. George here, he used to take on all comers in one of the tented booths. Don't think much of your fighting name though, George — Basher — Baggs. Not very imaginative.' He smiled thinly. 'But then, imagination was never your strong suit, was it? If it was, you wouldn't have been fitted up for that ram-raiding charge. Two years you got, was it? We never got our hands on the others. No way you were going to blow the whistle on them, to help yourself. Loyal, and stupid.'

'I don't grass,' Baggs muttered sourly.

'Then there was that bookie business at the Newcastle Races. You sort of rearranged his face.'

'He tried to welsh on me.'

'And regretted it later,' O'Connor surmised. 'After that, for a few years, there was a crop of petty stuff where you always seemed to come out worst. What they call the fall guy, really. Burglary, assault, drunk and disorderly, nicking cars, Paki-bashing. But then, this last six years, things have been pretty quiet really. Haven't heard too much about you. Changed your spots, George?'

'I got a job,' Baggs replied sullenly.

'Became a paid-up member of society,' O'Connor suggested with heavy sarcasm. 'Became domesticated. Even got a woman. Quite a woman, too. Where did you come across Jeannette Bartoli, George?'

The big man raised his head, stared at O'Connor with leaden eyes. 'She was working in a supermarket. I was shipping stuff in for her boss. She was in a bit of trouble at the time, there was this guy . . .'

O'Connor grinned. 'Discourage him, did you? And in gratitude, she moved in with you.'

'Something like that. Look, Mr O'Connor, all this is a big mistake—'

'Seems to me your life is a big mistake, George,' O'Connor interrupted. 'You don't seem to be able to keep out of trouble. And here you are again. In trouble. Tell me about this man Bovey.'

Baggs clenched his fists, his tone became edged with menace. 'That little shit. He came sniffin' around Jeannette when he knew I was away. Then I caught them at it. I gave him a hammering.'

'So we hear,' O'Connor agreed calmly. 'In hot blood: excusable maybe, if you catch your girlfriend in bed with another bloke. But Jeannette, she tells us you went after him again, a few days later. And this time, *really* gave it to him.'

George Baggs scowled. 'It wasn't like that. Jeannette, she sort of winds me up, you know? After I caught them, I gave him a few and her too. She promised it was nothing, it was over, and I believed her. But we got to having words again, because I wanted to know just what was in her head, why she needed to run after that little runt when I was away on the road, and she got mad and yelled at me and told me he was better than me, so I went around there again, to his house. If I'd found him, yeah, I reckon I would have really given it to him. But he wasn't there.'

'Jeannette says you killed him.'

'I'm no killer. I'm rough, but I'm no killer.' There was an odd tone to his protestation. It was as though he didn't really believe what he was saying.

O'Connor was silent for a little while. 'So you think maybe Saul Bovey got scared off, ran, doesn't want to know anything more about you and Jeannette. Gone to ground while he's still in one piece.'

'I reckon.'

'And he is still in one piece?'

George Baggs's eyes were careful. 'What do you mean?'

Casually, O'Connor leaned back in his chair, locked his hands behind his head. 'Ah, it's just something Jeannette told us. Let it slip, like. You had a quarrel again last night. Over the same thing, she says. Saul Bovey.'

'She kept on at me,' he agreed despondently.

'She shouted at you, told you she thought you'd punched him out, killed him.'

'I never—'

'And she says,' O'Connor interrupted, unlocking his fingers and leaning forward to confront the big man at the other side of the table, 'you yelled at her, said you hoped he'd been carved like the African kid.'

Baggs looked worried, he chewed at his thick lips, bruised and cut where his mistress had struck him. He touched his lip with a stubby finger, it came away marked with blood. 'I don't think I said that.'

'Your word against hers,' O'Connor said easily. 'But why would she make such a comment?'

He licked his finger nervously. 'We were yelling. She was crazy. I might have said something stupid.' Baggs was

126

sweating profusely now, a pale sheen spreading over his forehead.

'What do you know about the African kid, George?' O'Connor asked menacingly.

There was a short silence. Baggs shook his head slowly, like a half-stunned steer in a slaughterhouse. 'Look, I don't know nothing about that headless torso business. I was just letting off steam, just shouting the odds, she winds me up you know.'

'Someone phoned in to report the discovery of that African child's body,' O'Connor said quietly. 'In fact, there were three kids saw it first. They called this big guy, who came down and took a look and then told them to clear off. They told us he acted sort of funny after that. Seemed disturbed, shaken, uncertain what to do. But somehow, not surprised at what they'd found. That's what they said, George. Why wouldn't you be surprised?'

'It wasn't that,' he protested. 'It was just that I . . .' He stared blankly, suddenly aware of his slip. 'Aw, Mr O'Connor . . .'

'Those boys, they say they'd recognize the man again. It was you, wasn't it, George? You're the anonymous caller. Why didn't you just call us, and wait there? Why walk away from it?'

'I didn't . . .' Baggs was confused. 'Look, that wasn't the way of it . . . It was all her fault. I was near crazy, couldn't work out what to do. She was on at me, I knew she was two-timing me, and I beat that little bastard . . . And I took the Metro down to the coast, walked down along the prom at North Shields, getting some clean air in me lungs, trying to clear me head, think things out proper . . . but when I saw the black bundle the kids found, all I could think of was the blood, and my hands were sore, and . . .'

His voice trailed away. O'Connor frowned, watching him very carefully. 'Of course, it could have happened another way. The man who killed that boy, dismembered him, threw the torso in the river, he wouldn't have expected to see it coming back to him, on the Black Rocks at North Shields. It would have been quite a shock. Unhinged him a bit, shook him so he couldn't think straight, didn't know what to do. So he phoned in, but got away from there, fast.'

George Baggs straightened in his chair. He had been confused, shaken, destabilized by the collapse of his relationship with Jeannette Bartoli. But something happened to him now; some of the old stubborn steel came back to him, a native cunning that shone in his calculating glance. 'That's pretty wild, Mr O'Connor. There's no way you can prove that. I'm not a killer.'

The tremble had gone from his hands. Now they were bunched in front of him, on the table. There was a new confidence draining back into his veins.

Seated beside O'Connor, Raoul Garcia sucked at his teeth thoughtfully, and fingered his moustache. 'Mr Baggs, you said you met Jeannette Bartoli in a supermarket. You'd been delivering for her boss.'

Baggs's glance swept suspiciously towards the Interpol inspector. 'That's right. Booze and fags. Cheap stuff from the Continent. Everyone does it. It's just a game. He sold it on. It was just a side-line. Like I said, everyone does it.'

Garcia glanced quickly at O'Connor. 'So, Mr Baggs,' he asked Silkily, 'just exactly what was this job you were doing at the time?'

'Still doing it,' Baggs replied. 'Lorry driver. Long haul. Most everywhere in Europe.'

When Garcia glanced again at O'Connor there was triumph in his eyes.

* * *

Three days later a phone call came through for O'Connor. It was Dr Midgley, from the forensic laboratory at Gosforth. There was an odd note of relief in his voice.

'We got a match.'

'DNA from George Baggs?'

'Exactly. We picked up a smear of skin and blood from the black heavy duty plastic the torso was wrapped in. The analysis shows a match with the sample you gave us from Baggs.'

'This'll stand up in court?' O'Connor asked suspiciously.

'Absolutely.'

'You done a good job, Doc.'

'I'm just glad it's over.'

It was an odd thing to say, but O'Connor knew that the labs had been working at full tilt of recent weeks. Even so . . .

Raoul Garcia looked up from the files he was studying on O'Connor's desk. 'A result?'

'Looks like. DNA match linking Baggs with the torso.' Garcia nodded. 'I need to get on again to my office. It looks as though we've hit what you call the jackpot. If you can arrange for Baggs's employers to supply us with the man's time sheets, the routes he's been taking, the delivery points he's used, it looks as though we'll have a solution not to just one killing here in England, but maybe the Finnish student and the body the Dutch police found in the lake.'

O'Connor inclined his head in agreement. 'I've already started, it's in hand. So . . . you think Baggs might be the one.'

'He fits the profile, Jack.'

O'Connor wrinkled his nose in doubt. 'Yes . . . I see that. But somehow, I don't know . . . he doesn't leave me with the impression . . . I just don't see him as a serial killer, somehow.'

'Would any of us recognize one, if we saw him in the street?' Garcia countered. 'No, I think we have the man we want. I think we now know who did these terrible things. What we need to find out perhaps is, why?'

O'Connor shrugged and went back to his own paperwork. The thought returned to him, however, a butterfly fluttering in his mind. He was still puzzled by the almost palpable relief he had detected in Dr Charles Midgley's voice, at discovering the DNA match that could point to the killer of the African boy. It was as though Midgley had been taking the case almost personally.

It was unusual in a forensic scientist. Detachment was almost a necessary part of their make-up. It was a niggling thought that remained in the back of O'Connor's mind for the rest of the day.

CHAPTER FOUR

1

It was a busy time for the Department of Museums and Antiquities. Karen Stannard had attended the budget committee to determine the funding the department might expect to have available in the next financial year, but after its adjournment, with the request that further supportive papers should be presented, she absented herself from the department to go to Brussels, for discussions with James Stead regarding her proposed membership of the FCAI.

'Powell Frinton is very supportive,' she explained to Arnold before she left. 'He sees it as a feather in the authority cap, to have someone sitting on such a prestigious committee. And he agrees there should be no problems about you running the department in my absence. That's what deputies are for,' she added, favouring him with a flashing, insincere smile.

Portia Tyrrel was fully occupied now with the final work on the sea cave at Abbey Head. Dr Mwate was visiting there regularly, and Arnold suspected that Portia was consequently getting more enjoyment out of the work than she had done previously, an enjoyment that demanded her presence there every day. The opportunity to flirt with the big Zimbabwean was one not to be missed. Meanwhile, Arnold was left to deal with the budget in the finance committee. There were also the reports that needed to be finalized for updates on the geometric Roman mosaics that had been discovered at the ancient fort on Lea Fell and a survey of the hanging bridge that had been identified in a village north of Morpeth. It fell to him to deal with an application to be completed for a lottery grant to support the hunt for a seven-hundred-year-old fortress reputed to have been built near Alnwick to control the predations of William Wallace and Robert the Bruce. And then there was the matter of attendances at meetings to discuss the new government strategy to modernize and financially support regional museums, such as those that came under the control of Karen's department.

He knew now why he had never wanted her job.

At the end of several hectic, grinding days Arnold was glad to see Karen return, so that he could escape into the fresh air, and visit the Fordbridge site. It was gratifying to see that work had proceeded apace. The access road for Joe Holderness's housing estate was still creeping up the hill but the archaeological team were now clearing the medieval site completely, and the Iron Age chariot burial was almost ready for final documentation. He was interested to note that the medieval complex had thrown up another unsuspected location: a well, its sides walled with cut stone, almost filled, naturally enough, with rubbish and domestic waste, unused for perhaps four hundred years. But the team had already dredged up a number of artefacts: leather shoes, decayed documents, pottery shards. The well had been excavated to a depth of ten feet so far, and there was every evidence that it might go down to forty feet or even more. Arnold was pleased that Holderness had agreed to delay his takeover of the site: the chariot burial was the most important activity on site, but the newly discovered pit would run it a close second. There was still much work to be done, and he immersed himself in it for the next week.

And it was good to be back up on the hill. The blue distant fells were sun-streaked, cloud-dappled. The breeze sweeping in from the coast had a clean, fresh, salty tang to it. He felt relaxed, free from the burdens of the office work as he assisted in the excavations at the burial site, and when the Tornado jets — three of them — shrieked their way across the sharp blue sky just two hundred feet above their heads it was only a briefly thunderous irritation. Nevertheless, the rolling crash of their passing meant that he failed to hear the car coming up the hill on Holderness's access road.

When he heard the car door slam he turned, shading his eyes with his hand, half expecting it might be Karen. It was not. He made out the lean figure of DCI O'Connor, walking up the hill towards him.

As he approached, O'Connor raised a hand in greeting and glanced around at the group working on the site. 'It's getting along then.'

'Quietly,' Arnold agreed.

'In spite of the jets.'

'Young men training to save us from the dictators of the world. I just wish they'd do it a little less noisily.' O'Connor nodded. 'Ah, well, boys will be boys — even in million quid jet planes.'

Arnold brushed some of the dirt off his hands, rubbing them against already stained jeans. He narrowed his eyes against the sunlight as he looked at the detective. 'So, what brings you up here, Mr O'Connor? Finding time to relax, now you seem to have sorted out the murder of the African boy?'

'What makes you say that?' O'Connor asked quietly, turning his head to fix Arnold with a cool glance. 'According to the newspapers you've made an arrest, and a man's been charged. I assumed . . .'

'Aye, well, we've charged someone.' O'Connor seemed hesitant, about to say something more, then thought better of it. 'We'll see how it goes.'

'So is this a social visit or is it police business?'

The policeman shrugged, shoved his hands into his pockets and looked around at the expanse of the site. 'Bit of both, you could say. Partly curiosity, I suppose. I hear that you've managed to pull some extra funding for the excavations, from the Holborn Trust.'

'Through its funding committee, that's right.' O'Connor wrinkled his nose, and nodded thoughtfully.

'That'll be the committee Miss Stannard will be joining soon. I had a word with her,' he explained, 'in your Morpeth office before I drove up here.'

'I see,' Arnold replied, though he did not.

'I called into the office but it was you I really wanted to have a chat with, not Miss Stannard.'

'Really?' Arnold was surprised.

'You know much about the committee?' O'Connor asked in a casual tone.

'The FCAI? How do you mean? I know what it does, naturally.'

'Well, not so much its work . . . more, the people who comprise the committee.'

There was a distant drone, from a fighter jet, tracing a white vapour trail high above their heads. Arnold watched it for a moment, then shrugged. 'I've met them, of course: the chairman, James Stead, Dr Mwate, Dr Midgley, Professor Forray, Dr Woudt . . . Why do you ask?'

O'Connor made no reply for a moment. He walked slowly across to the edge of the excavations, inspected the recently discovered well, turned and watched the young university student from Mwate's department scraping away at the clay surface with a small hand trowel. 'Painstaking . . .' he murmured, almost to himself. He turned to glance at Arnold. 'Is this what Dr Midgley came up to see the other day?'

'Dr Midgley?' Arnold's brow wrinkled in thought. 'He was here last week, yes. It was a sort of general visit. He hadn't seen the site earlier — though Dr Woudt had been up here previously, the day we heard about the FCAI grant. The FCAI committee is part-funding the project, so I suppose he wanted to check it out for himself. Make sure the money was being used appropriately, that sort of thing. He got quite enthusiastic about it.'

O'Connor nodded distractedly. He raised his head, looked around the site, up towards the beech trees on the hill, glanced up at the sharp blue of the sky. 'What did Midgley talk to you about, when he was here'?'

Arnold stared at O'Connor, not knowing quite what to say.

* * *

Midgley's arrival the previous week had been unexpected and unannounced. He had reached the site some fifteen minutes after Arnold, and had bustled over, self-importantly, anxious to look over the work that had been going on. Arnold had shown him the excavation itself, and taken him into the hut where the artefacts that had been discovered were stored, in the process of being catalogued. Midgley had nodded in approval. He had been surprised to learn that there had been an additional recent discovery, the medieval pit, and he enthused over it, recognizing that there might be interesting material to be recovered from such a find. 'An additional bonus to what we had already decided to fund,' he chuckled.

In both manner and attitude, he was different. When Arnold had met him first at the Carcassonne conference the forensic scientist had been friendly enough, imbibing freely, chatty, outgoing. During the formal part of the conference Arnold had seen little of him, but from a distance he had seemed to be ebullient, sociable. But after Arnold had picked up the document case by mistake, and left it at Midgley's bedroom door, the man's attitude had darkened. Karen had already remarked upon Midgley's clear dislike for Arnold. In the rasping phone call from Midgley that dislike had been all too apparent, based as it was on a foolish mistake Arnold had made.

But now, as they walked around the site, things seemed to have changed. Midgley was relaxed, more like his previous self, and he seemed to bear no animus towards Arnold. Indeed, shortly before he left, he had put a friendly hand on his arm, squinting up at Arnold in the bright sunshine as he apologized.

'Look here, Landon . . . I think I need to set things right.'

'In what way?' Arnold asked warily, remembering Karen Stannard's warnings.

Midgley smiled deprecatingly. 'Well, I think I sort of went off the deep end at Carcassonne. When I found that document case outside my room and read your note of explanation, I kind of, well, hit the roof. I felt . . . when I looked at what the case contained, I took it as a personal insult that you would even think that I . . . well, you know, would be interested in that sort of disgusting stuff.' He wrinkled his nose in distaste. 'I got rid of it immediately, of course.'

Arnold had felt embarrassed. 'No, I suppose it's I who should apologize. It was stupid of me. It's just that when I saw the photographs, I had a bit of a shock, and then I thought, with your forensic background, maybe it was something to do with a case you were working on . . . I repeat, it was stupid of me.'

'I appreciate that,' Dr Midgley said, blowing out his cheeks in a sigh of relief. 'The fact is I was upset at the time, and the matter rankled with me — things have been pretty hectic at the labs, and, well, you know how it is . . . Anyway, a lot of issues have been sorted out now, and I just feel I was taking out on you certain problems . . . It's just one of those misunderstandings, well, you know what I mean, don't you?'

Arnold didn't, but thought it best to agree.

Charles Midgley linked his arm through Arnold's. 'So, Arnold — may I use your first name? We'll probably be working together from time to time on this funded programme so, no bad feelings, hey? Water under the bridge, all forgotten, over and done with, that sort of thing. I'm sorry I was so abrupt with you.'

'That's fine with me,' Arnold replied. After all, he agreed they had a working relationship to develop.

They had walked around the site for a while, discussing the findings, Arnold taking the opportunity to gently disengage himself from the arm linking. It seemed just one friendly step too far. Then as they walked back towards Midgley's car the forensic scientist had put his hand on Arnold's arm again.

'Just one thing, Arnold,' Midgley suggested confidentially. 'That document case . . .' He grimaced as though the thought of it gave him pain. 'It's already caused a certain embarrassment, a misunderstanding between us. It could obviously cause other . . . misunderstandings. If it became known that it . . . well, even existed, it might raise problems, cause questions to be asked. I got rid of the damned stuff. Burned the lot . . . so I don't think we need make any further reference to it. Not between ourselves. And certainly no need to mention it to anyone else. Best the whole matter stays buried, don't you think?'

Arnold hesitated. 'I've no real problem with that.'

'So mum's the word, as they say. No one else needs to know about that little bit of unpleasant business, hey?' Charles Midgley heaved a sigh, in relieved satisfaction, a burden lifted from his mind. 'Let's move on. After all, we have this endeavour ahead of us: stupid to hold grudges. And with Karen coming on to the committee . . .' The mention of Karen clouded his brow. He glanced at his watch. 'Hell, I've got to move. I've another appointment.' For a moment a shadow seemed to cross his face, then he brushed it away, nodding at Arnold. 'I really must go. But I've enjoyed the visit and I look forward to working with you over the Fordbridge site . . . and maybe others in the future, hey?'

* * *

That was last week. Now, a chattering helicopter hammered its way above their heads and O'Connor looked up to the sky. 'You reckon we'll see some more Tornadoes in a while?'

'Probably. They have regular runs across this valley. Maybe they'll stage a mock attack on the chopper. They sometimes seem to undertake exercises in tandem,' Arnold explained.

O'Connor nodded, folded his arms, glanced around at the site thoughtfully. 'So you're telling me that Charles Midgley just came up here to talk to you, take a look at the work his committee was funding. And when he was here, he seemed pretty relaxed, at ease with himself.'

'That more or less sums it up,' Arnold agreed.

'And he said he was looking forward to working with you and Mwate and Woudt on the Fordbridge site.'

'In so far as he would be able to spare time from his work at the forensic labs. That's what he said.' Arnold was vaguely uncomfortable. He had not disclosed to O'Connor the differences that had arisen between himself and Dr Midgley at Carcassonne, or even the existence of the pornographic material he had picked up by mistake in someone else's document case. Midgley had said it was over and done with. Arnold saw no reason to raise the matter, particularly since it would seem to have been resolved.

He watched O'Connor as the policeman folded his arms and paced about, walking in a tight, thoughtful circle. 'So as far as you could tell, Charles Midgley didn't seem to have anything on his mind, anything troubling him?'

'Not that I could detect.' Frowning, irritated by the way in which O'Connor seemed to be harping on about Midgley's appearance and manner, Arnold asked, 'Just what's this all about, Mr O'Connor?'

The detective chief inspector hesitated, clicked his tongue, then glanced at Arnold quizzically. 'What's it about? I'm not sure. All I can say is, you seem to be the last person to have had a conversation with Dr Midgley before he . . . went missing.'

'Missing? I don't understand,' Arnold muttered, confusion in his voice.

'He'd completed some work for us on the African boy last week. He rang in with some results, DNA information, then apparently left for home. After that it seems he didn't turn up again at the labs. We needed certain confirmations and rang in to the pathology department the next day, but the police liaison officer told us Dr Midgley had not been in to work. We weren't too concerned at the time, thought maybe he was not feeling well, or was taking some time off, or was involved with FCAI activity, but then, well, we called his home. No answer. We sent a car around there. All locked and barred. He's a widower, you know. Lives alone.'

'I didn't know.'

'Not really important.' O'Connor frowned. 'Anyway, after a day or so we checked with FCAI and elsewhere, but nothing turned up. It seems as though Dr Midgley has sort of . . . disappeared.'

'His colleagues weren't able to help?'

'They had no idea what had happened to him. We looked at his diaries, but they weren't much help. But someone recalled he'd gone to see someone at the Department of Museums and Antiquities. We checked. Karen Stannard told us he'd certainly called in at her office, spoken to her last week, just prior to coming up here to see you and look over the site.' His glance fixed on Arnold, contemplatively. 'After he saw you . . . nothing.'

Arnold shook his head, unable to think of anything to say.

'You've no idea where he went after he saw you?'

'None. Is it important?'

'Well, we've completely lost track of his movements after he visited you here. You say he told you he had an appointment.'

Arnold nodded. 'He seemed to be in a hurry — anxious to get away.'

'You know who he was meeting?'

'He didn't mention any names.'

DCI O'Connor jingled the keys in his pocket in a distracted manner. 'We found his car in the car park at Newcastle airport. It was in a time-restricted zone. He clearly had not expected being there long. Was that where his meeting was scheduled, do you think?'

Arnold shrugged helplessly.

O'Connor resumed his pacing. 'So, what have we got? You tell me nothing seems to have been troubling him. He seemed relaxed, he was looking forward to working on the Fordbridge project, everything seemed to be fine — and he was hurrying off to keep another appointment. With an unnamed person.'

'That's about it,' Arnold agreed.

Carefully, O'Connor asked, 'Do you think this meeting he was going to, it could have been something to do with FCAI?'

'I've no idea,' Arnold replied. 'As I said, he didn't tell me who he was going to meet, or where the meeting was to be. And as far as I'm aware, Fordbridge is the only project in this country that the FCAI is funding . . . or intends to fund for the time being. So . . . why do you think it might be FCAI business?'

O'Connor heaved a deep, frustrated sigh. 'Ah well, that's another thing. Midgley, he's not the only one who seems to have disappeared.'

'I don't understand.'

O'Connor grimaced. 'We've not been able to trace the whereabouts of another member of the FCAI.'

'Who are you talking about?' Arnold asked in surprise. 'Dr Martin Woudt.' O'Connor bared his teeth in a wolfish grimace. 'Like Dr Charles Midgley, another member of the FCAI committee seems to have vanished from the face of the earth.'

2

Sid Cathery was clearly a man who believed in a hands-on approach. O'Connor found it irritating. It was not that he himself was a loner, or inclined to hug information to himself as a source of power, but conferences with the Assistant Chief Constable were not one of the better management practices he had come across. They smacked of interference. Instead of letting the men get on with their jobs, Cathery insisted on being involved, kept up to date with each step in the progress of the investigations.

It was probably just another form of pressure, O'Connor concluded. And unsubtle, at that.

The Assistant Chief Constable settled back in his chair, interlaced his fingers and let his frosty glance drift over the men in front of him: DCI O'Connor, DI Farnsby, DS Robinson, and, seated to one side of the group, Inspector Garcia. Cathery's voice was bleak, his tone wintry. 'Right . . .' he drawled. 'Let's see how far we've got . . . or not.' His eyes rested on O'Connor, as the senior officer. 'You want to begin, DCI?'

'In respect of the murder of the African boy, we're still pursuing the various lines of enquiry, sir.'

'Various lines?' Sid Cathery's brow clouded. 'But you've already made an arrest. This man Baggs—'

'That's true,' agreed O'Connor, 'but George Baggs still insists—'

'That he's innocent,' Cathery interrupted, 'but they all say that, don't they? Damn it, O'Connor, you've got DNA, haven't you?'

O'Connor hesitated. 'That's right. The forensic lab came up with a match, but I've been looking again at the details. And I've discussed it with some of the people at the CPS—'

'Those spineless incompetents,' Cathery grunted contemptuously. 'What the hell do they know except how to delay an investigation?'

'The fact is,' O'Connor continued doggedly, 'we do have a match but the specimen of blood and skin came from the outside of the torn heavy duty plastic that the torso was bundled in.'

'So?' Cathery growled, unwilling to concede but with his eyebrows ridging darkly.

'The torso had been tied up in the heavy duty plastic, and thrown into the river . . . or possibly the sea.'

'The sea?'

O'Connor nodded. 'The amount of salt deposit There's a possibility it was dumped at sea, and it was the tides brought it up on the Black Rocks area, rather than coming downriver. We know it was Baggs who found the torso, after those three kids called him down to the rocks. He's admitted that, now he's scared enough. And the kids have identified him, anyway. But forensic found no DNA traces matching up with Baggs, not inside the bag, nor on the body itself. Only on the outside of the plastic. When he touched the material, and saw the torso, Baggs's hands were raw. From the beating he'd given this man Saul Bovey. The CPS are doubtful it's enough. The defence will argue the DNA came from his dragging at the plastic when he found it. There's no DNA link to the torso itself.'

Cathery's features were sour. 'What about this Bovey character?'

'It's as we guessed. After he got hammered by Baggs for the second time — the tale Baggs told us about Bovey not being there when he went around wasn't true. He was there all right and got thumped. Bovey only scarpered after the second beating. He'd decided the game with Jeannette Bartoli wasn't worth the candle. I think he knew if Baggs had got hold of him again, he would have killed him: he was mad enough. Anyway, after that second thumping Bovey got the hell out of Benwell. We traced him eventually, holed up in Fort William, nursing his wounds and his pride.'

'Scotland?' Cathery grunted in contempt. 'He'd run far enough.'

'He felt it best to keep his head down, and keep a distance between himself and our ex-pug Baggs.'

'Is he going to bring charges?'

'He wants nothing more to do with the Bartoli woman, or Baggs.'

'And you've got doubts that we've enough evidence to tie Baggs in to the killing of the boy.' Cathery slowly unlinked his stubby fingers and contemplated them for a little while in displeasure. Eventually, his glance flickered towards Raoul Garcia. 'What do you think about all this, Inspector?'

Garcia straightened in his seat. The fingers of one hand caressed his moustache. 'I don't wish to dispute with my friend DCI O'Connor. But I still think we have the right man in Baggs. It may well be that we have no direct evidence linking him with the torso, but I have been talking to his employer. George Baggs works for a Middlesbrough-based firm called InterHaulage Ltd. This man Baggs has been travelling, driving the firm's lorries, making deliveries across most of Europe. It was because he was away so much that Jeannette Bartoli turned for consolation to this man Saul Bovey.'

'What's all this got to do with the African boy?' Cathery queried irritably.

Garcia shrugged, he waved his hand in deprecation. 'No direct link . . . yet. But we have been working with various colleagues who have been conducting separate investigations in Holland and Germany. My colleagues in Bruxelles and

I, we have a strong feeling that there are links between the killings under investigation in Europe, and the discovery of the torso in the Tyne. We believe we have a serial killer on our hands, who takes souvenirs. Like heads, and feet.' His glance flickered around the room, gauging the silence. 'It is perhaps no more than a coincidence that George Baggs has been driving his lorry through Germany, Holland, Finland, Italy . . . It is perhaps no more than a coincidence that killings have taken place in areas where he has driven. Killings where gruesome souvenirs have been taken. But . . . well this is one of the lines of enquiry DCI O'Connor was referring to. We are now trying to pin down dates for the travels undertaken by Baggs . . . And we are also checking for further DNA evidence.'

'You have some DNA from the European murders?' Cathery asked sharply.

Garcia nodded. 'We're now trying to find a match.' Cathery settled back in his chair and looked again at O'Connor. 'So we might yet link up Baggs with the killings in Europe as well as here. But you still have an open mind.'

O'Connor twisted his mouth in uncertainty. 'It's just that I feel for the moment we don't yet have enough on Baggs.'

'Bloody hell O'Connor! You've charged him!'

'That might have been a bit premature,' O'Connor admitted, colouring slightly. 'And the charge is obstructing justice, not murder.'

'All right then . . . What about this *muti* thing?' Cathery asked crisply.

'Still looking at it.' O'Connor hesitated. 'But we've hit a bit of a snag. I've decided to use Dr Mwate no more.'

Cathery cocked his head on one side like a predatory bird eyeing its prey. 'Why's that?'

O'Connor scratched his chin doubtfully. 'We've dug up an old file. On advice. It relates to an incident over twenty-five years ago.' He glanced at Farnsby. The DI raised an eyebrow, knowing where the advice had come from. 'There was a bit of a fuss. a family in Fenham raised the alarm about a missing child. There was talk of ritual killing. Then it all died down, and the family went back to Africa. We thought at first it was Nigeria, but it wasn't. They were from Zimbabwe. So . . .' He held Cathery's cold glance. 'I think it, perhaps . . . unwise to use Dr Mwate any further. It may be he's . . . compromised by earlier events.'

'Compromised? You've lost me. What the hell are you talking about?'

'The Zimbabwean family was called Mwate,' O'Connor explained stiffly. 'Consequently I think it's maybe unwise to continue using Dr Mwate as a consultant. There's something fishy about the business involving his family back in the seventies.' He paused. 'But that doesn't mean we've ruled out this *muti* theory. It's still a possibility that ritual was involved in the killing of the African boy. And it's still a possibility that there's something in the argument that the limbs and head were removed for use in *muti*.' He cleared his throat uncertainly. 'Rather than to prevent identification. We're just not ruling anything out, not yet.'

'What you mean is, you're getting bloody nowhere,' Cathery growled unpleasantly.

Garcia stepped in hastily, to help out. 'We are pretty certain, sir, that the boy came in from somewhere in Europe. So there are matters we are following up there. The evidence of the shorts manufacture is something we are pursuing.'

Cathery sighed. 'But you still think it's all down to George Baggs. God, I feel like we're running in circles here. All right, so we've got Baggs but it isn't yet all over . . .' He turned his chair slightly, fixed his glance on DS Robinson. 'And the Starlight Club?'

Robinson flexed his burly shoulders and licked his lips. 'The CPS have the files now, sir. We've got a strong case against each of the guys we've taken into custody. Charges have been filed. And we've now been able to confirm—' he glanced at Garcia and nodded his appreciation '—through our friends at Interpol, that there's a European network that the local website of the Starlight Club was tapping into. So the whole thing is wider than we'd anticipated.'

'But concentrating on the Starlight Club itself, the UK operation, you got *all* of them in the net?'

An edge of nervousness came into Robinson's tone. 'We still haven't identified The Doctor, but we're getting there,' he muttered defensively.

'Sooner, I trust, rather than later,' Cathery muttered sarcastically, then turned his head, contemplated DI Farnsby. 'And now my own pet little hate. How are you getting on with Don Catford?'

Farnsby shifted uneasily in his chair under the Assistant Chief Constable's scrutiny. 'We don't have a great deal to go on, sir.'

'But . . . ?'

Farnsby sighed. 'We've been around there. His showroom at South Shields. Put a bit of pressure on. We're checking his movements. We've run his car registrations through the computer. We've been looking at cargo lists on the Hull-Zeebrugge and Hull-Rotterdam ferries. We've planted two men on the most recent runs.' He looked Cathery boldly in the eye. 'I gather they quite enjoyed their overnight crossings, sir.'

Cathery's lip curled at the challenge. 'If I truly detect from your tone that you think checking out Catford is a waste of time, let me give you a different point of view, Inspector. I've looked closely at the file, from the point of the raid on his garage business months ago. We know the enquiry was closed down, ostensibly for lack of evidence, but more probably because Catford started screaming harassment, pulled strings in high places. But let me tell you, categorically. I *know this man*.'

The silence in the room was edged with unease. Farnsby's cheeks were pale.

'Don Catford is scum,' the Assistant Chief Constable said with emphasis. 'There isn't a criminal activity or a dirty bit of business that he wouldn't get into, if he could make a profit out of it. You've seen his record—'

'Not many actual convictions, sir,' Farnsby resisted. Cathery glared at him, annoyed at the interruption. 'Only a few convictions, but a hell of a lot of justifiable suspicion. He's no fool, is Don Catford, he's jumped ship a few times before it sank under him, but I tell you, his downfall will be that he's *greedy*. There'll be more than one scam he's into, I'm telling you. I know him of old. If we can nail him on this doctoring of cars and shipping them into a distribution network in Europe and elsewhere, I'm certain we'll uncover all sorts of other nefarious villainy. If we could get into his computer bases, the filth that will come spilling out . . .' He stopped abruptly, suddenly aware of the heightened tension, the electricity in the air. He was sweating lightly, moisture on his upper lip. He brushed it away with a finger, aware he had been on the point of being carried away by old enmities. He took a deep breath, glared sourly at Farnsby. 'So keep the pressure on the bastard. That's official.'

Farnsby nodded, his features expressionless.

The silence grew around them, broken after a while by Sid Cathery's fingers drumming impatiently on the table in front of him. 'So that leaves just one more thing,' he suggested, flickering a glance at O'Connor.

'Dr Midgley.'

'No information yet?'

Jack O'Connor shook his head. 'We've talked to everyone at the labs. We've looked at his diaries. We've turned his house over. We've checked with his neighbours. We've spoken to the man who, as far as we know, was the last person to see him.'

'Anything suspicious there?'

'None. It's a man called Landon. Midgley visited him at the Fordbridge archaeological site, they talked about the dig, but Midgley left him there, said he had another appointment, and we've traced Midgley's car to Newcastle airport. It was in the restricted zone, near the hotel. Probably that's where he had the meeting he mentioned to Landon. As for Landon's own whereabouts, we have independent confirmation of his movements, from the work force on site.'

'Newcastle airport. We're not dealing here with a man who's just gone on holiday, I trust,' Cathery suggested sarcastically, 'leaving his car at the hotel and flying off to Majorca or something?'

'No, sir,' O'Connor replied levelly, 'we've checked with the airlines flying out of Newcastle. No record of Midgley flying out. And we're not looking at a possible suicide, either. We've spoken at length to the people who were in touch with Midgley in the days before he disappeared, both at the forensic labs and elsewhere. His state of mind was not suicidal, as far as they could make out. He had certainly been under a deal of pressure, not least from us over the African boy's killing, because we were desperate for results. And it's been suggested he was worrying about that — he was certainly worried about something. People say he's been a bit withdrawn, concerned, uncommunicative . . . But the last few days before his disappearance, he seemed to everyone to be more relaxed, more cheerful . . .'

'Since he discovered George Baggs's DNA?' Raoul Garcia intervened.

'That might have been it,' O'Connor agreed. 'Pressure off his lab . . . An apparent solution to a problem. But of course, we also have the disappearance of Dr Woudt to contend with.'

'Woudt? And who the hell is he?' Cathery demanded. 'Dr Woudt served on a funding committee with Charles Midgley. The FCAI. So does Dr Mwate, for that matter.'

'And?'

'Well, it's a bit odd that Midgley and Woudt seem to have disappeared on the same day, more or less. We've been on to the Rijksmuseum. It seems Woudt had recently tendered his resignation from the post of curator there. And he also resigned from the FCAI. Then — he just disappears. As does Dr Midgley.'

'You think there's a connection?' Cathery asked, chewing at his lip.

'It remains to be seen, but it's certainly a bit odd,' O'Connor suggested.

'I've been in touch with Bruxelles,' Raoul Garcia added.

'There is no local file on Dr Woudt. One would not expect one on such a respectable person. But Interpol are extending the search, and are now trying to trace him in Europe.'

'Whereas we need to concentrate on Dr Midgley.' Cathery's tone was raw with frustration. 'Just what the hell is going on here?' He glared around at the group of silent men. We need to get some answers soon — we have to tie Baggs firmly into the killing of the African boy, find out who the hell The Doctor is, and trace Dr Midgley.' His glance rested on DI Farnsby. 'Never forgetting Catford . . . never forgetting that slimy bastard!'

* * *

Noel Penworthy was proud of his war record. He had served as a naval gunnery officer on a frigate in the Royal Navy during the Second World War, and had seen action in the Mediterranean. In some ways, that period had been the high-light of his life, a time when the excitement and tension and danger had seemed to make him exist on a different, sharper plane. He felt a little of those old emotions now, as he stood in the afternoon sunshine while the group of men worked on the bank up to his right. He felt *involved* again.

'But you know,' he said to the stolid constable standing beside him on the green bank, looking down to the black winding course of the stream at Seaton Sluice, 'when it's all over they forget you, they don't want to know. I've been writing to the War Office, you know, because I'm gradually growing deaf. It was the guns in the war, that's obvious, and I deserve compensation. It was the guns that did it. My hearing's getting worse and worse.'

The police constable glanced at him wearily, took in his stooping shoulders, desiccated frame and wisps of white hair. 'Just how old are you now, sir?'

'Eighty-two. But until recently I could hear fine. It was those guns . . .'

And certainly, there was still nothing wrong with his eyesight, at least, not since he had had an operation for cataracts. It was all just as he had explained, after his phone call, when they had come out to see him at his house.

'Normally, you know, I just take Timmy — that's my golden retriever there — I just take him for a walk along the headland down there, just opposite the pub, down to the harbour, sit for a while, see what boats are coming into the little moorings there. Not much can, of course, it's so small, but it was important once. The Delavals of Seaton Delaval Hall built the harbour, you know, in the seventeenth century, to export coal and salt. Big coal owners they were, the Delavals. They cut right through the rock to make a new entrance for the sluice, and a deep-water dock . . . Aye, normally I just walk Timmy down there.'

They had been forced to wait while he rambled on a little further.

'But once a week, usually, I give him a change. Instead of a run along the beach while I watch from the headland, and then a quiet sit-down on the bench overlooking the harbour, I take Timmy across the road bridge and up the valley. It's nice along there, you know: flat banks of green land you can walk on, water birds in the black water of the sluice, and the stream sort of winds along, twisting and turning between its narrow cut. Further on up the valley there's a castle, you know, they say it's haunted, but Timmy and I don't usually go that far. And on the right bank, it sort of slopes up and there's scrub and trees and you can startle all sort up there, or Timmy does, anyway, pheasants, oyster catchers, teal, widgeon, duck . . . But when he started digging like fury under the trees, I was surprised. He loves chasing the duck and the gulls, does Timmy, but digging, no. And there's nothing wrong with my eyesight, you know, even if the guns have affected my hearing. Did I tell you I've been writing to the War Office? They won't even answer my letters about compensation . . . No, my eyes are good. So even from a distance I could see he'd come across something funny . . .'

Penworthy had rubbed at his watery eyes. 'Aye, he was digging, and I could see it was something odd, like an arm . . . and a hand. He came away when I whistled, though. He's a good dog, Timmy . . .'

* * *

O'Connor experienced an intense repugnance, visiting forensic pathology laboratories. He loathed the atmosphere of such places, the faint odour of formaldehyde. There was a morbidity about the laboratories that was not dissipated by the attitude he seemed to detect among the staff. Often relatively young people, they tended to indulge in horseplay, exchanged laboured jokes, shared a brittle, black humour. He knew it would be their way of dealing with a career that involved grisly dismemberment, the probing of bodily cavities; the analysis of fluids and juices, hearts and lungs and livers. But he always felt an intestinal shudder when he entered such a laboratory.

This occasion was somehow different.

There was a subdued air about the laboratory as he entered. The man who came forward, extending his hand in greeting, was in his late thirties: he introduced himself as Dr Saunders. He led O'Connor along the corridor, where they were joined by the police liaison officer. At the entrance to his office, Saunders hesitated, seeming a little nonplussed. O'Connor became aware that a nameplate had been removed from the door itself.

Saunders waved them to take seats. He was a thin-faced, youthful-looking man, with flaring nostrils and sad eyes. At the moment he seemed distinctly uneasy.

'Can I offer you some coffee?'

'I've already organized it,' the liaison officer said quietly. Dr Saunders picked at his fingers as though seeking an irritating split nail. He glanced about him, at the filing cabinets, the books on the shelf. 'This all seems a bit premature, moving in here, but they said that as the deputy I ought to start using the office, until appointments get properly sorted out.'

O'Connor grimaced. 'So there's no doubt about it?'

Dr Saunders shook his head despondently. 'We all hoped, of course. But when the body was brought in from Seaton Sluice, even though the head and face had been badly beaten about, and decomposition was well advanced, there was a sort of feeling . . .' He took a deep breath. 'We have our own defence mechanisms, you know, DCI. We all have our own individual ways of dealing with what we have to face in the lab. The worst is when we have to talk to grieving relatives. It's not a duty many of us are prepared to volunteer for. The rest of the time, we . . . are indifferent, or seem to be. But when it's one of our own . . .'

'The identification is certain?'

Saunders nodded soberly. 'The body that was found at Seaton Sluice by Mr Penworthy is undoubtedly that of Dr Charles Midgley.'

There was a short silence. The liaison officer cleared his throat. O'Connor turned his head as a white-coated staff member brought in a tray with cups of coffee. He was silent until she had gone. 'Are you able to give us any information about cause and time of death yet?'

Saunders reached out and toyed with the handle of his coffee cup. 'It's too early to present full reports, of course. But there are certain things we can conclude.' A shadow crossed his eyes. 'Charles was beaten to death: something like a tyre iron, would be my guess. The blow which crushed his skull would have been enough in itself to kill him, but the person . . . the perpetrator then proceeded to rain further blows, on his face. Almost frenzied, I would say.'

'Time of death?'

Saunders shrugged. 'Last week, but maybe up to ten days ago. It's difficult, because the nature of the soil on the bank at Seaton Sluice . . .'

'We have him fixed on the thirteenth at Fordbridge, then his car was parked at the airport hotel the same day.'

'That would probably be the day he died.'

'Was there anything of significance on the body?'

Saunders frowned, pursing his lips thoughtfully. 'All clothing had been removed. I've been left with the feeling that the killer probably intended leaving as few clues to identity as possible — the beating of the head, the removal of clothing — but perhaps he was disturbed, or perhaps he was in a hurry. Maybe couldn't finish the job he intended.'

O'Connor was silent for a little while, he sipped his coffee contemplatively. It was better than the slush that got served at Ponteland. He raised his head. 'What's the chat in the labs?'

'I beg your pardon?'

O'Connor held the man's glance until it dropped. 'There must have been some discussion among your colleagues. Whys and wherefores. Apart from the clinical discussions, I mean. Midgley was one of your own. What did you know of Midgley's private life? Were there any names that might have cropped up?'

Saunders shook his head. 'There has been some conjecturing . . . but nothing meaningful. Charles Midgley was a widower, a private man, he had no real friends at the lab. He was the senior officer . . . and he kept very much to himself, really seemed to live for his work. His only outside interest was his archaeology, really, he saw the two interests as complementary. He . . . he was very proud of his membership of the FCAI. He was very . . . protective of it, even. Perhaps it was something to do with FCAI that caused him to seem preoccupied of late.'

'How do you mean?'

Saunders frowned thoughtfully. 'I'm not sure. You'll be aware he visited Carcassonne, the FCAI conference there. When he came back, something seemed to be worrying him. He didn't discuss it with any of us. I guessed it was something to do with his membership. He regarded his committee membership as a high honour. I can't say . . . it was just an impression, but to me he seemed to value it so highly that he would never let the FCAI be sullied, you know what I mean?'

'Not really,' O'Connor considered.

Saunders clucked his tongue in frustration. 'I can't express it better. It was . . . just an impression. And in any case, he seemed to have got over it, latterly. He was brighter the last time I saw him, more like his old self. So it was all resolved, I suppose. Before he went missing.'

O'Connor drained his coffee cup. 'You have the photographs for the file?'

Saunders nodded, reached into the desk drawer, extracted a folder. 'They don't make good viewing. However . . .'

'Yes?'

'I don't know whether you've been told yet.' Saunders glanced at the liaison officer, who shook his head.

'Told what?'

Saunders hesitated, scratched at his lip. 'When Mr Penworthy's dog found the burial place, scratched at it, there was some disturbance, of course. Your scene of crime unit cordoned it off, and we started work — the complete exhumation, the investigation of the site. Because of the disturbance, our people then extended the search area a little. That's when we found it. We're now widening the search area further.'

'What did you find?' O'Connor asked, somewhat irritated that he had not already received the information.

'This.' Saunders extracted a photograph, handed it to O'Connor.

'What is it?'

Saunders wet his lips with a nervous tongue. 'It's an ankle bone. We also found some metatarsals . . .'

O'Connor wrinkled his brow, puzzled. 'Dr Midgley's?'

'No. The bones we've found, some ten or twelve feet or more from Dr Midgley's interment, they would have belonged to a child. What you're looking at is the decayed foot of a seven-year-old child, Mr O'Connor.' There was a slight, unprofessional tremor in his voice when he added, 'We're expecting to find more.'

O'Connor stared at the photograph numbly. 'Are you telling me . . . ?'

'The child,' Saunders stated in a flat tone, 'was black.'

3

The morning sunlight glittered and danced on the rippling surface of the river. The waters had risen in the uplands of Mont Lozère at an altitude of fifteen hundred metres and had forced their bustling, turbulent way down through the slopes of the Cevennes into the Causses region. There the river had carved its way through a series of rifts, deepened over the millennia into steep-sided limestone canyons, dolomite gorges where the sun beat down relentlessly in summer and through which the river in spate had been known to wash away villages and hamlets in spectacular flash floods. But here, at Sainte Enimie, the river was now more relaxed, placid, chuckling its way through the arches of the bridge, accepting with equanimity the group of muscular young yellow-jacketed men and women who were setting out in their kayaks, to explore the reaches of the Gorges du Tarn.

The village of Sainte Enimie lay in terraced rows below the steep cliffs which bordered a loop in the Tarn where the canyon itself was at its narrowest point. The retaining walls rising in tiers from the banks had for hundreds of years boasted vines, and almond, walnut, cherry and peach trees, but for the last forty years the terraces had gradually fallen fallow, the result of a population exodus, leaving the remaining residents to make a living from tourism.

From where they stood on the narrow medieval stone bridge spanning the river, O'Connor could see the entrance to the track that led to the cave-hermitage reputed to have been used by the seventh-century Merovingian princess Enimie, who had been miraculously cured of leprosy by the healing spring of the Source de Burle, now a place of pilgrimage where numerous similar miracles were said to have occurred. But O'Connor's eyes ignored the track. His glance was concentrated on the solitary figure of the man seated in the sunshine on the terrace, outside the cafe overlooking the river. He was reading a newspaper, sipping coffee, unaware of the two burly young men in open necked shirts who were casually taking up seats at a nearby table on the sunny terrace. Above their heads a flock of pigeons nestled on the roof of the cafe, warming themselves in the sun, cooing softly in satisfaction.

O'Connor glanced at Raoul Garcia. 'Shall we go down?' Garcia smoothed his moustache, nodded, and checked his watch. 'I think all would now appear to be in place, my friend.'

O'Connor waited as Garcia dropped the half-smoked cigarette and ground it under his heel. They took their time as together they strolled across the bridge towards the tiny village square. They were both dressed casually and could have been taken for tourists. The season itself was almost over but there were still holidaymakers travelling the gorges, seeking the views from Point Sublime and Rocher de Capluc, taking advantage of the river trips from La Maléne, hiring kayaks at Sainte Enimie.

They crossed from the river bank and took seats on the cafe terrace, at the empty table next to the man with the newspaper; he remained immersed in his reading. After a few minutes, the middle-aged waitress came out, flirted her eyelashes at Garcia, then took their order. '*Deux cafés — un café crème, un normal.*' The man beside them shuffled the pages of his newspaper but did not raise his head.

Raoul Garcia leaned forward. 'Good morning.'

The reader looked up. He wore a pale lemon Armani shirt, a cream cravat, light-coloured, sharply creased trousers, tan Gucci shoes. The sunlight glinted on the gold rims of his sunglasses. Reluctantly, he nodded. '*Bonjour, messieurs.*' He lowered his head again, returned to his scrutiny of the newspaper.

'You are reading *Le Monde*,' Garcia observed in English.

'That is correct,' the man replied. His own English was easy, slightly accented, but he made no attempt to hide a note of mild irritation in his voice. Clearly, he resented being interrupted.

'I see they have made a breakthrough,' Garcia commented, gesturing towards the headline on the front page. 'Russian lorry driver questioned in serial slayings,' he translated, for O'Connor's benefit. His dark eyes shifted towards O'Connor, and he gave a little shrug, almost of apology. The man beside them glanced at the headlines, then hunched forward slightly, ignoring the comment.

They sat in silence for a while, until the waitress had returned with their coffees. She gave Garcia a brilliant smile, ignoring O'Connor. Garcia took a lump of white sugar, dipped it into his coffee and crunched it with evident satisfaction. He was very much at ease with the world. He did not look at the man on the next table as he said, 'You are well?'

They could not see the man's eyes, masked by the dark lenses of his sunglasses, but as his head came up it was clear he was surprised, and his irritation was growing. '*Bien sûr,*' he almost growled, and lowered his head once more.

'Ha, that is good, that your health is strong,' Garcia replied complacently. 'My friend and I here, we had heard otherwise, you see.'

There was a pause. Slowly, the man raised his head again, stared at him, his body very still. Then he clearly decided to ignore the comment. He shrugged, reached for his coffee, drained the cup and began to fold his newspaper. He started fishing in his pocket for some coins.

'I believe you are staying in one of the apartments up there on the hill,' Garcia said casually, glancing behind him.

'In the restored medieval village. What number is it . . . thir-ty-seven, yes? You have owned it for some years, I understand. Was it your mother, or your stepfather who first bought it, before you acquired it on their death? A splendid place to come to stay, to recuperate, if you are not feeling well.'

An elbow jerked involuntarily and there was a rattling sound as a spoon fell from the table. The man with the sun-glasses sat rigidly, staring in sudden bewilderment. 'How did you . . .' Whatever he was about to say, he suddenly reconsid-ered, his mouth shutting like a trap. After a few moments, he muttered, 'I told you, I am feeling quite well. And you will excuse me, but I must leave now.'

'Well, don't go back to the apartment just yet,' O'Connor intervened. 'We'll be wanting to take a look at it shortly.'

'All the relevant documentation has been completed,' Garcia assured him.

The man rose slowly to his feet, his body stiff, his movements uncontrolled. The hand holding the newspaper quivered slightly, the slim fingers trembling. 'What are you talking about?' he asked in a low voice. 'Who are you?'

Garcia raised a deprecatory, apologetic hand. 'Ha, it is remiss of us. So impolite not to make the necessary intro-ductions.' He waved an elegant hand. 'My colleague here is Detective Chief Inspector O'Connor, from Northumbria, in England. My name is Garcia — I work for Interpol.' He nodded past the standing man to the table nearby. 'And those two gentlemen, they are French detectives. *Flics*.' He smiled in friendly fashion. 'They are there to help out, just in case any difficulties arise, and they are waiting for several more of their colleagues, who will be arriving shortly to search the apartment you've been using. It's been quite an international operation to find you, Dr Woudt.'

The man in the pale lemon shirt seemed rooted to the spot. His tongue flickered over dry lips. He cleared his throat nervously. 'I'm afraid you've made a mistake.'

'No mistake,' Garcia replied with reassuring confidence.

'There must be. My name is Steiner. Alex Steiner.'

'Ha, yes, that was what we found so interesting. Steiner . . . that is the name under which you own the house. But it is also a name that you were accustomed to using so many years ago, when you got into what my friend here would describe as a little hot water.'

'I don't know what you're talking about,' the man insisted, but suddenly his legs seemed to weaken and he sank back into his seat.

'It's been quite a problem,' Garcia assured him earnestly, 'trying to trace you. You covered your tracks well. When you disappeared, after resigning from the Rijksmuseum, no one seemed to be able to help. Nobody had a forwarding address. There were no clues left behind at your apartment in Amsterdam. You had simply vanished into thin air. But, coincidentally, in pursuing other enquiries a curious fact came to light.' He glanced at his companion.

'We've been making enquiries into a group of rather unpleasant people in England,' O'Connor advised. 'They've been operating under the name of the Starlight Club. We've had them under arrest, but there were a few loose ends, including the identity of one of their number. So, we extended the enquiry, not least when it became apparent that the Starlight Club had been networking with a European organization with similar objectives, and tastes. And that's when we came across something very interesting. A fact which eventually, and really surprisingly easily, led us to this village.'

As he watched Martin Woudt's reaction, O'Connor's thoughts swept back to the meeting with Sid Cathery in the Assistant Chief Constable's office. 'So what's this all about?' Cathery had growled.

Garcia had been flushed with excited pride. 'We have managed to discover some most important links, with regard to Dr Martin Woudt,' he announced. 'We think we can make out at the very least an indirect bridge between him and your investigation into the Starlight Club.' He jabbed with his finger at the folder in front of him. 'Enough at least to justify our questioning him.'

'I thought you hadn't been able to trace Woudt.' Cathery had grumbled, raising his eyebrows.

'We think we know where he is now,' O'Connor had insisted. 'A little place called Sainte Enimie in the south of France.'

'I have to admit it was largely a slice of luck,' Garcia admitted, with a modest smile. 'When my colleagues extended the search into paedophile networks in Europe — following up your search for The Doctor — they came up with a name. You know how it is in investigations, eighty per cent sweat and twenty per cent luck. This time, luck was on our side. One of our young researchers, he had come across a name on the register of paedophiles — a young academic called Steiner, who had been arrested and charged with certain offences some ten years ago. His name and mug shot were on the files, but our bright young researcher, he also happened to see the photograph that had been circulating in the search for Dr Woudt. There was a discrepancy of some years between the two photographs, naturally, but our young man has a keen eye. He recognized a certain similarity between the photograph we had provided for Interpol — the one of Martin Woudt — and the photograph held on the offenders file. The department ran a computer check on the young Steiner's file and came up with the fact that Steiner's birth certificate was actually in the name of Woudt. Martin Woudt's mother had married a second time. Her first husband, Martin's father, had died when the boy was seven. The second husband was called Steiner. Martin Woudt was brought up using that name, though his birth records were still in the name of Woudt.' Garcia paused. 'Enquiries also brought to light that there had been a prosecution, when the boy was eleven. It seems the stepfather had been abusing the child . . .'

Sid Cathery frowned. 'So Steiner — Martin Woudt or whatever — had been abused as a child. Where does that leave us?'

Raoul Garcia shrugged with a hint of despondency. 'It's a classical situation. A child is abused. He himself becomes an abuser, in later life.'

'But he must have escaped that stigma,' Cathery argued, 'If he was able to obtain the job of curator at the Rijksmuseum.'

'He covered up the situation, after his early conviction, by reverting to the name of Woudt. The name of his real father. He became a respectable academic. But it's highly likely he never got rid of his tendencies.'

'Why do you say that?' Cathery demanded with a frown.

'Because the name of Steiner not only appears in the criminal records from ten years ago. It also appears in the list of people involved in the European network. The people who had been in contact with the Starlight Club group.'

There had been a ruminative silence. Cathery had glowered at Garcia. 'This is all very well . . . and circumstantial. But unless we can question this man . . .'

'We think we know where he is,' Garcia countered swiftly. 'The records show that when his stepfather was imprisoned for offences against the boy, the mother moved to an apartment in the village of Sainte Enimie. Old man Steiner disappeared for a few years after his release from prison and is believed to have died in a car accident in Biarritz. The mother herself died some years ago and left the place at Sainte Enimie to her son. In the name of Steiner, which she had never changed in spite of her second husband's offences.'

Cathery shook his head. 'You'd have thought she'd have wanted shot of the name . . .'

'Maybe. But she never did,' Garcia insisted. 'We've made enquiries in France, and it seems the apartment in the village is still held in the name of Steiner. And there is a man staying there right now.'

'Woudt?' Cathery asked crisply.

'We think so.'

'I think you should authorize Robinson to get across there immediately, sir.' O'Connor suggested. 'Inspector Garcia has made all the necessary arrangements through Interpol, and the French police have been alerted.'

'Will they agree to our dragging him back here?'

'It's not a question of extradition at this stage, sir, we just want the chance to talk to Woudt but the French police will want to take a look at him also, in the matter of their own enquiries into the European paedophile network. Dr Martin Woudt may be able to give us the answer to several of the questions that have been concerning us, sir.'

'You mean with regard to the killing of Charles Midgley?' Cathery growled.

'That,' agreed O'Connor, 'and there's also the link with the Starlight Club.'

'*Doctor* Martin Woudt,' Cathery grunted with heavy emphasis. Then he shook his head. 'I see where you're heading. If this really is Woudt, staying in France under the name of Steiner, we need to talk to him. But . . . I don't know.'

He stared at O'Connor for a few moments, deep in thought. 'I'm aware that Robinson is in charge of the Starlight enquiry, but we need someone more senior to go over there with Inspector Garcia. Also, with the possibility of these links . . .' His cold eyes glittered as he made his decision. 'You'd better accompany Inspector Garcia yourself. Robinson stays here. And O'Connor — bring us back a result. We sure as hell need one right now.'

'The use of your stepfather's name, it was an extremely useful cover, was it not?' Garcia suggested easily, leaning back in his chair, sipping his coffee.

Slim fingers toyed nervously with the collar of the lemon shirt, straightened the cravat that did not require straightening. 'I must insist . . . I don't know what you're talking about.'

'The charade is pointless, Dr Woudt,' O'Connor said quietly. 'We know who you are, and how you managed to cover your tracks, coming here. And maybe, once our French colleagues have taken a look at what you've got in the apartment here at Sainte Enimie, well, who knows?'

Martin Woudt was silent for a little while, then he shrugged his narrow shoulders. 'You will find nothing . . .

incriminating in the apartment. You are free to search it, as far as I'm concerned. I have nothing to hide.'

'So why are you on the run?' O'Connor demanded.

'Am I?' Some of his earlier assurance had crept back into Woudt's manner. 'What makes you assume I am . . . on the run, as you put it? This apartment belongs to me. I am entitled to use it. I have no commitments at the moment. Do I have to account to anyone for my movements? Or for the use of the name under which I was brought up?'

O'Connor leaned forward, his glance boring into Woudt's eyes. 'We've spoken to your chairman at the FCAI, James Stead. He tells me your resignation from the committee was very sudden — and unexpected, as far as he was concerned. You told him it was on the grounds of ill health.'

Woudt made no reply, but shrugged contemptuously. 'But you now tell us you're quite fit. And we've also been in touch with your employers at the Rijksmuseum. Your resignation there was equally sudden — and to them, just as inexplicable.'

Woudt touched the rims of his sunglasses, adjusted them carefully with his fingertips. 'I need explain these things to no one. They were my decisions. I was . . . bored.'

'I don't think so. Not bored, scared.'

Martin Woudt sighed and removed his sunglasses. He extracted a white silk handkerchief from his pocket, began to polish the lenses thoughtfully. 'What you suggest is nonsense. What do I have to be scared of?'

'Exposure.'

There was a short silence. Martin Woudt took a deep breath. 'You say the *flics* have authority to search my apartment. That is fine. They can go ahead. They will find nothing of interest to them. You, Mr O'Connor, have taken the trouble to come here from Northumberland. You, Mr Garcia, from Brussels or some such God-forsaken place. I am afraid you have both had a wasted journey. There is no reason why I should talk with you further. I have nothing to say to you. Now, if you will excuse me—'

'I'm afraid you still don't understand,' O'Connor said harshly, putting out a warning hand as Woudt began to rise again to his feet. 'We're not interested in dredging up the past, looking at your early life, or even checking what false references you might have used to pursue your academic career, or get the job at the Rijksmuseum, or take up membership of the FCAI committee. We're interested in more recent events.'

'Such as my resignation from the Rijksmuseum? Hardly a heinous offence,' Woudt sneered.

Garcia's eyes were cold. 'No hanging matter, for certain. But I suppose you are aware that at about the same time you went missing, Dr Charles Midgley also disappeared.'

Woudt's features were impassive as he slowly slipped the sunglasses on again. He glanced up at the sun, as though testing the lenses. 'I was not aware that Charles had been . . . missing. There has been no report in the French newspapers. I am sure he will have a full explanation when he reappears. If he is inclined to give one, as I am not in respect of my own movements.'

'Ah, but that's the difficulty,' O'Connor replied in a quiet voice. 'I said he'd disappeared. But we actually found Dr Midgley before we traced you here to Sainte Enimie.'

'You found him?' There was a hint of strain in Woudt's tones. 'So what then is your problem?'

'The problem is the circumstances of his discovery. We found him buried in a shallow grave. Near the riverbank at a place called Seaton Sluice.' He paused. 'Would you happen to know the place, Dr Woudt?'

Woudt made no reply. His mouth seemed to have slackened, his breathing irregular.

'He had been beaten to death, it seems,' Garcia added.

'Very messy,' O'Connor agreed.

Woudt still said nothing, but he had paled.

'We wondered what you might be able to tell us about his death,' O'Connor continued.

Woudt found his voice. His tone was strangled, indignant. 'I? What on earth do you think I can tell you? I don't know what you're getting at!'

'I'm pointing out the fact,' O'Connor countered in a reasonable tone, 'that you were a colleague of Charles Midgley on the FCAI committee. There's also the fact that shortly before he disappeared, you resigned from the FCAI committee, at a time when Midgley appeared to have been worried about something. The next fact is that Midgley seems to have recovered his good spirits . . . and made an appointment to meet someone. After which he vanished. And so did you. And we've discovered his body. These are the facts, Dr Woudt.'

'And you are like a spider, spinning a web of circumstance from these facts,' Woudt scoffed sarcastically, with a sudden surge of nervous confidence. 'But what are you spinning, in fact? Nothing but insubstantial cobwebs in the air.'

'You don't seem to realize you are involved in a murder enquiry, my friend,' Garcia murmured softly. 'One from which it is possible you might be able to extricate yourself, if you answer our questions satisfactorily.'

'Questions, questions,' Woudt snapped irritably. 'You cannot be serious, suggesting I can tell you anything that will help in discovering who might have killed Charles Midgley. He was a fellow committee member, a friend of mine. I am distressed at receiving this news about his death. But I was not even in England when he died—'

'We don't exactly know when you left England,' O'Connor suggested. 'We're assuming you left, perhaps, after keeping an appointment with Charles Midgley at Newcastle airport.'

'That is an incorrect assumption,' Woudt replied coldly. 'When did this . . . meeting take place?'

'When did you leave England?' O'Connor countered.

Woudt glared at him, fingers twitching on the table in front of him. He shook his head. 'This is a silly game, nothing more. I think we shall conclude the discussion now. If you want to talk to me again, I think it should be through my advocate. You are seeking to entrap me. You are not even acting within your own jurisdiction. This is France, not England, and I don't have to put up with this interrogation.'

Garcia smiled gently. 'What you say is true. Neither I nor Mr O'Connor have any powers here. But we had hoped you might be able to allay any suspicions we might have, with a frank and rational explanation. But, if you please . . . The situation is, if you don't talk to us now, informally, help clear up some matters, we will be applying for extradition papers, to bring you back to England to face formal charges. The French police have certain enquiries of their own to make, concerning your alleged membership of a European network tied in with the Starlight Club in England, so you will be held pending those enquiries being completed. That will give us time to apply for extradition. So you will not be at liberty. You will not be able to flee again, you will not be able to use such other names as you might have access to, in order to escape.'

'I use no other names,' Woudt replied sullenly. 'And extradition . . . you could get that only if I actually had charges to face.'

'Oh, there are possible charges,' O'Connor assured him grimly. 'Serious charges.'

'I cannot believe it,' Woudt said stubbornly, but his unease was emphasized by the nervous tic in his cheek 'Murder? The killing of Charles Midgley? You must be making a big joke! What you are saying, it is ridiculous, it is illogical.'

'I regret to say that from your point of view, we have a great deal of logic on our side,' O'Connor insisted, shaking his head.

Woudt raised his chin, defiantly. 'So tell me! Give me the result of your logic, your ridiculous deliberations!'

Garcia glanced at O'Connor, raised an eyebrow. O'Connor nodded.

'Why not? Let's take it step by step, logically, and see what you think, Dr Woudt, about our . . . as you put it . . . ridiculous deliberations. Let me put it as a sort of scenario.'

Woudt snorted in contempt, but he leaned forward nevertheless, his concern obvious.

'We know,' O'Connor continued, 'that Charles Midgley, amateur archaeologist as he was, set great store by his membership of the FCAI committee. We've been told he was very proud of it, and indeed was very protective of its reputation.'

'So?' Woudt questioned uneasily.

'So at some point — we've yet to determine when, and how — Dr Midgley became aware that one of the FCAI members was likely to bring scandal down upon the committee.'

Woudt bridled. 'Are you suggesting—'

'He found out that you, Dr Woudt, have been active in the dissemination of pornographic material involving child abuse through a European network.'

'That is a lie!'

'Your name exists on a register as a result of your conviction under the name Steiner, years ago,' Garcia advised blandly. 'And Interpol have now come up with names of people in the network Alex Steiner is among them.'

'Steiner is a common name,' Woudt blustered.

'So it is,' O'Connor agreed gently. 'But may I continue with my scenario? Let us assume I am right, that Dr Midgley discovers your guilty secret. What would he do about it? First, he would be anxious and worried that the scandal of your exposure would bring the FCAI into disrepute. He would be uncertain what to do. We have evidence from his colleagues that he certainly seemed upset in the days before his disappearance, worried about something.'

'I have no knowledge—'

'But then what he must do becomes clear to him. He must confront you. He must act so as to prevent damage to the committee, and maybe the Rijksmuseum also. The avoidance of scandal. So, on one of your business visits to Tyneside — what is the business that draws you there anyway?'

'My business is my own affair,' Woudt muttered defensively.

O'Connor shrugged. 'We can pursue that later. But on a recent visit to Northumberland, perhaps when you visited the Fordbridge site, Charles Midgley contacted you, met you, warned you that he knew about your . . . tendencies, insisted that you resign from the FCAI, and resign also from your post as curator at the Rijksmuseum. If you did not do so, he said he would expose your activities, give evidence against you, see you jailed . . .'

A light sheen of sweat glistened on Woudt's forehead.

He shook his head. 'This . . . what you say, it's all nonsense.'

'You took his warnings seriously. You contacted James Stead, told him you were resigning from the FCAI on grounds of ill health. You then spoke to your employers, and resigned unexpectedly from the job at the Rijksmuseum. This was a considerable relief to Charles Midgley. It was after you agreed to resign that his mood lightened, he became more like his old self. A burden had been lifted.'

'I do not know about all this,' Woudt blustered.

'But then you paid one more visit to England.'

Woudt took a deep breath. He glanced over his shoulder, as though to confirm the presence of the two French policemen. His mouth writhed unpleasantly. 'I don't have to listen to this . . . It is a charade, it is—'

'Too near the truth?' O'Connor interrupted. 'What was it that drew you back, to meet Midgley again? Was it that he wanted something more from you? Or was it simply that, having reflected upon what you had done, you felt resentment, wanted to get revenge upon him? Or did you arrange the meeting at Newcastle airport because you realized that your secret would never be safe with him, that the deal you'd struck — resignation, for his silence — was too chancy, that he might expose you anyway?'

'None of this is true!' Woudt insisted desperately.

'We think you met him at the airport. You drove him in your car, under some pretext or other, away from the airport, leaving his car behind. And then you attacked him, beat him with a car jack or something similar. And you buried him, in a hastily dug, shallow grave at Seaton Sluice.'

Woudt ran a hand over his forehead, it came away damp with perspiration. He stared at his hand, it was shaking. 'This is all supposition. You can prove nothing of this. You are trying to scare me. You tell me Charles Midgley is dead. You say I killed him. I deny this. I deny knowing anything about Dr Midgley's death.'

'But it's not just the killing of Charles Midgley, is it?' O'Connor suggested casually.

'What do you mean?'

'We've discovered that it wasn't just Dr Midgley who was interred near the river bank at Seaton Sluice. We found the other remains also. A foot. Decomposed flesh, leg bones, arms . . . we're still searching for the head . . .'

'I don't know what you're talking about!' Woudt's voice had risen, almost to a wail of disbelief.

O'Connor's tone was steely. 'I'm talking about a headless torso that was found in the Tyne. An African boy, about seven years of age. Murdered. Dismembered. It seems we've found much of the rest of his body. Buried at Seaton Sluice. Only a matter of metres from the body of Charles Midgley. Surely, you'll agree, Dr Woudt, that cannot be a matter of mere coincidence!' He leaned back, fixing Woudt with an icy glance. 'And now we've found these coincidental links, there's one other matter that seems to slot into place. The Starlight Club.'

Woudt was shaking his head, but his mouth was panicked. 'All this . . . murders . . . I deny—'

'We've arrested all the members of the Starlight Club, apart from one. We've not been able to discover his identity. Over the network, he's identified only as The Doctor. But now, we're beginning to suspect maybe we've found him. We think the separate investigations we've been carrying on, they're actually linked. It's all so logical. *Doctor* Martin Woudt!'

'This is incredible!' Martin Woudt hissed. 'You cannot prove any of this. You cannot saddle me with a charge of murder. You are searching the wind. You are making wild accusations.'

'You're saying all of this is incredible?' O'Connor sneered. 'Believe me when I say I think we'll be able to prove you killed Charles Midgley, had a hand in killing the African child, were involved with the Starlight Club as you were in the European network, and we are pretty certain we can identify you as The Doctor!'

'No!' Martin Woudt was almost beside himself. He rose to his feet in sudden panic, thrashing his arms about, almost turning over the table as he stood up. The two policemen behind him started to their feet, moving forward as Woudt raged at O'Connor and Garcia. 'All this is what you call a frame-up! What you say is not true. Don't you understand me when I tell you?' He slammed one hand down on the table in front of him.

The flock of sun-somnolent pigeons on the roof rose, scattering, fluttering furiously above their heads, panicked as the man below them almost screamed the words. '*You're talking to the wrong man!*'

CHAPTER FIVE

1

'Would you believe it? He's gone and changed his bloody mind again!'

Karen Stannard stamped around her room, almost beside herself with rage. Arnold glanced at Portia Tyrrel, standing meekly beside him in Karen's office, and waited. He knew what the problem was, in fact, he had received some forewarning of it. Joe Holderness had spoken to him on the telephone that morning. He was too gruff to be apologetic, too bluff to say he was sorry. But he had explained things to Arnold.

'It's because the country's going to the dogs, that's what. First of all the bloody banks can't make up their minds. One minute they lend you even more money than you really asked for in the first place, fall over themselves to give you what they call lines of credit, and then suddenly get lily-livered, worry about overdrafts, and start calling in loans. Then there's all this terrorist business, and the collapse of the stock market. What do they expect me to do? I've got all my spare cash locked up in property, plant, machinery — I can't afford to sell what shares I've got. The banks demand I reduce the overdrafts, so if I don't get the next phase of the building work done, and keep the sales team active, I'm deep in the proverbial mire. So I've got no choice,' he had grumbled. 'I have to complete the next phase. I know I said I'd hold off for a few months, but things have changed. I'll be giving instructions in the morning and the bulldozers will be moving up the site.'

Arnold waited as Karen continued to pace the room like an angry tigress. If she had a tail, he thought irreverently, she'd be swishing it. 'The old bugger,' she snarled in fury. 'He waited until we'd put up the hoardings with his company name prominent on them, he held off until he'd got all the mileage he could out of the newspaper coverage, he had his day basking in the sun of publicity, and now he tells me he's withdrawing from the agreement. Men!' She glared at Arnold as though he epitomized the species, or were somehow involved in a plot to undermine her. 'You just can't trust them. Ever.'

Carefully, Arnold submitted, 'From what I gather, Joe Holderness has little choice. He's under considerable financial pressure from the banks.'

'He's been talking to you?' Karen snapped suspiciously, whirling on him, stabbing a finger in his direction. 'There you are, it's what I mean! Little boys clinging together.' Arnold thought it best not to respond. Her claws were unsheathed, and he did not care to face a verbal ripping he did not deserve.

'Just what does it mean as far as the site is concerned?' Portia asked.

Karen returned to her desk still fuming, sat down, glared at the sketch map spread out in front of her. She took a deep breath, calming herself. 'Fortunately, it doesn't bring everything to a halt. From what Joe Holderness tells me, he's going to be driving the access road up here, on the western edge of the dig. That means we'll still be able to carry on — though for God knows how much longer, with him changing his bloody mind all the time — with the medieval complex and the chariot burial.'

'The cart site is still viable for us then,' Portia corrected her description.

Karen shot her an angry glance. 'Cart, chariot, wagon, whatever. You really ought to get a life, Portia, and not niggle about such detail. We get a better press if we call it a chariot.'

'And publicity is important. Yes. But from the sketch map—'

'It's the new find that's at risk. The well—'

'The pit, yes,' Portia murmured.

Karen expelled her breath angrily. She glanced at Arnold, murder in her dark eyes, but for once it was not directed at him. 'The ancient *pit* falls in direct line with the edge of the access road. Within two days, three at most, we will have to abandon the site as Holderness earth-moving equipment moves in. That means we'll have to get our skates on if we're to gain maximum benefit from the find. And we'll need all the manpower we can get hold of. Maybe the university can help.'

'I was talking to Dr Mwate yesterday, at the sea cave,' Portia mentioned casually, leaning over to inspect the sketch on Karen's desk. 'I don't think we'll be able to obtain much assistance from his students. They've all been withdrawn from Abbey Head now, because of impending examinations. My guess is he won't be able to get them along to Fordbridge, to help out.'

Karen swore. She flashed a frustrated glance in Arnold's direction. 'Everything seems to be collapsing about us suddenly. Holderness . . . work on the site . . .' She hesitated, her thoughts flickering away from the immediate difficulty at Fordbridge. 'I suppose you've heard about Dr Midgley?'

Arnold grimaced. 'It was in the newspapers yesterday and on the TV news. They've discovered his body, and it seems the burial site up at Seaton Sluice wasn't used just for him alone. There are other remains also.'

Karen nodded soberly. 'I was on the phone with James Stead this morning. The FCAI is in a state of uproar. Midgley murdered. Dr Woudt resigned. Stead was moaning to me about it all. Telling me about all the problems it raises for the committee.'

'Will his concerns affect the funding?' Arnold asked.

Karen shrugged. 'I hope not. But he was complaining as though he regretted having made the offer of financial support for Fordbridge in the first place. He seemed to imply that the decision somehow had brought bad luck to the committee.'

'More than just bad luck, as far as Dr Midgley was concerned,' Portia commented blandly.

She was out to wind up Karen Stannard's already tight springs, Arnold guessed. It seemed she took every opportunity to do so these days. As the thought crossed his mind, he heard Portia ask, 'Do you think all this trouble at the FCAI, Karen, will affect the proposal that you become a member of the committee?'

Karen glared at her. 'It's not a terribly important consideration at this moment,' she lied, 'what with all the other issues facing us. Charles Midgley had been given the task of monitoring the project, so the FCAI will have to find someone else to do it now. It can't be me, obviously, even if I join the FCAI as planned. It can't be Martin Woudt, because he's resigned for whatever reason — and until the FCAI identify another member who'll have time to oversee the project, there'll be difficulty in releasing the necessary funds they've promised us.' She rubbed a frustrated hand over her furrowed forehead. 'And now you tell me Dr Mwate can't help with his students, when time becomes of the essence.'

'What about our own departmental staff?' Arnold asked.

Karen shook her head, grimacing. 'All committed elsewhere, or on leave, or sick . . . I've never known a time like it. And we've got a couple of days . . .' She leaned back in her chair, surveyed her room as though for inspiration, shook her head. 'There's only one thing for it. We three are going to have to roll up our own sleeves, and get our hands dirty. For as long as it takes . . .'

They started work that very afternoon.

* * *

While still being aware of the time pressure placed on them, and reminded of it by the increased activity on the Holderness building site below them on the hill, Arnold found working at the dig enjoyable. The weather was kind to them, a light breeze blowing in from the coast, intermittent sunshine under white scurrying clouds. The two women were professionals, and whatever personal problems might lie between them, when they got down to work on the pit site they worked in tandem, complementing each other perfectly. Arnold was in the pit itself for most of the time, filling baskets with the contents of the pit, raising them to the edge of the well, for Portia to sift them more finely and carry interesting matter across to the hut where Karen sorted and cleaned and marked for identification. They did not finish until it was almost dark. The back of Arnold's thighs ached from the unusual exercise, climbing up and down the ladder into the pit, so he was glad when they then drove down to a pub in the nearest village and managed to get a reasonable, if somewhat basic meal and an indifferent bottle of wine in the lounge bar. They agreed to meet up at the site again early in the morning, Karen driving Portia, while Arnold would make his own way to Fordbridge independently.

He felt dog-tired, back and legs aching still when he tumbled into bed. He fell asleep quickly. Some hours later he woke again, with a start. He glanced at his bedside clock. The glowing figures showed him it was after three. He lay in the darkness, turning uncomfortably, oddly ill at ease. His pulse was uneven. Vague anxieties crowded into his mind. He remained where he was for a while. He could not be sure what had wakened him, a dog barking, an unexpected noise in the garden outside, perhaps an urban fox, but he was left with an unreasoning, obscurely disturbed feeling. And it was not the first time. The last few days he had felt uncomfortable, a prickling of the hairs at the back of his neck, the feeling that somehow he was not alone, his movements being watched.

After a while he rose stiffly, put on a dressing gown and went to the window, looked out into the darkness. A pale sliver of moon gleamed intermittently, half-hidden by dark rolling clouds, and he could see little. He padded through to the hallway, turned on the porch light and again looked out through the window but there was nothing untoward to be seen. Anything could have woken him, he reasoned, maybe it had been a car passing the end of the quiet road where he had lived now for some years, maybe it was just the nervous excitement of the day. And the feeling of discomfort . . . it was probably just his imagination.

Or perhaps it was the jumble of disconnected thoughts that were still floating through his mind in the dark hours. Charles Midgley, Carcassonne, a document case containing pornographic material, and a violent death. The thought came back to him, persisted, that he should perhaps have mentioned the events at Carcassonne to DCI O'Connor when he had had the opportunity. Now . . .

He returned to bed, but his sleep remained fitful.

Just after six he gave up attempting to rest further, rose, showered, dressed and after downing a quick cup of coffee he set out for Fordbridge.

The good weather of the previous day was unlikely to return, he guessed. The morning sun was obscured by the dark clouds piling up on the horizon as he made his way towards the site. The breeze had strengthened and there was a hint of rain in the air, misting upon his car windscreen. There were people moving about on the Holderness building site but Arnold was the first to arrive at the Fordbridge dig and he quickly got to work, unrolling the length of tarpaulin that had been used to cover the pit, protecting it overnight from vagaries of the weather. He rolled it up carefully, set it to one side. He looked up at the sky, it was likely they'd have to use the covering before the day was over.

He had just climbed down into the pit to begin sifting when he heard the car arrive, crunching over the rough track that would soon become Joe Holderness's access road. A car door banged, there was the sound of feet trampling into the hut, and a few minutes later Karen Stannard was looking down at him from the edge of the pit.

'You've made a start, then.'

'Just.'

'Okay, Portia's here with me, so we can get on with things quickly. We brought some stuff with us for lunch so we don't need to leave the site. You see the forecast this morning?' When Arnold shook his head, she added, 'Rain throughout the north, and gales this evening. We're going to have to move fast, Arnold, the fates and the weather are conspiring against us.'

They carried on the process they had begun the previous day.

Karen had a mug of coffee in her hand a couple of hours later when she appeared at the edge of the pit and called down to suggest Arnold joined them, took a break. Arnold climbed the ladder out of the pit and joined the two women in the hut. Karen looked up and down at Arnold, critically. 'You look a right mess.'

'It's pretty muddy down there,' he explained, glancing down at his stained jeans regretfully. 'If we see any rain today, we'll have to move fast to get the tarpaulin on, but even then there'll be seepage into the pit. I don't see how we're going to get this job finished in time.'

'Well, we will be getting another pair of hands,' Karen said as she handed him a mug of steaming coffee. 'I've just had a call on my mobile from Dr Mwate.'

'He's coming up to the site?' Portia queried, brightening somewhat.

Karen's glance was suspicious. 'He apologized for not being able to bring any students with him, but he said he'll try to get here before lunchtime, to help out.'

'All hands to the pump, hey?' Portia commented, smiling, making no secret of her pleasure that the big Zimbabwean would be joining them.

He arrived within the hour, just as the first light shower of the day drifted over the fell.

2

The house in Gosforth was Victorian, set back in a quiet cul-de-sac, double-fronted, four-storeyed. The area was reckoned to be one of quiet gentility, faded respectability, but the houses were certainly far beyond Farnsby's financial means. His, or anyone else's on the force for that matter, with the likely exception of the chief constable, or his deputy.

When he had received the phone call from DCI O'Connor, Farnsby had immediately made his way to Sid Cathery's office and had quickly received agreement to get a search warrant for the house in Gosforth. The magistrate had been compliant, and within two hours they were parked at the end of the cul-de-sac, two police cars, five men. But when Farnsby rang the doorbell there was no response. He waited, rang again, while the men behind him shuffled impatiently.

It was clear there was no one at home.

Farnsby hesitated. A search warrant was one thing, breaking and entering was another. He looked back at the men standing behind him, and he recalled the urgency in Jack O'Connor's tones. The DCI was flying back immediately, but would not be in Newcastle for some hours yet, and there was reason to believe the man they sought was desperate. He sucked at his lip, then stepped back.

'Break it down.'

'Sir?'

'You heard me. We're going in.' And to hell with the consequences, if they were wrong.

The door splintered under the heavy, ringing blows. a few minutes later, Farnsby was climbing over the wreckage to find himself in a long, narrow hallway, his boots echoing on Victorian tiled floors. He snapped his fingers, motioning two of the men to climb the stairs. He himself prowled through the high-ceilinged lower rooms with a detective constable in tow. In the comfortably furnished sitting room a half-empty bottle of whisky stood on the coffee table, a puddle of brown liquid still in the glass that accompanied it. There was a degree of untidiness about the room: rumpled cushions, newspapers strewn on the floor, television set on standby, not properly switched off. Farnsby frowned. There was an atmosphere of anxiety in the room, impatience, uncertainty. He heard one of his men call out down the stairs. 'No one up here, sir. One room's been occupied — bed unmade.'

Farnsby considered matters, the hairs tingling at the back of his neck. Charles Midgley was dead, Dr Woudt in hiding, and here a man had been pacing, cursing, anxiously deciding what next had to be done. DCI O'Connor had been specific in his terse instructions: get to the house, drag the man in for questioning, and do it *fast*.

But for the moment, the bird had flown.

Farnsby flipped open his mobile, called the number O'Connor had given him. The connection was quickly made.

'O'Connor. What's happening?'

'The house is empty,' Farnsby replied. 'Where are you?'

'Still on the road. We managed to get a flight into Heathrow but it'll be a few hours yet till we get back north. Have you been right through the house?'

'Most of it. Nothing significant yet. But what do we do about him?'

O'Connor cursed roundly. 'From what Dr Woudt has told us, my guess is he's not finished yet. I doubt that he knows we're on to him, but he's panicked, trying to cover all eventualities, get rid of any links . . . We've got to think, Farnsby. The names of the people at the Carcassonne conference, people Midgley might have talked to . . .'

The line crackled, and the connection was broken. Farnsby hesitated, waited for a while, tried the number again. There was no service.

He wandered out of the sitting room. He could hear the men upstairs, moving furniture, not certain what they were looking for. Two officers were in the kitchen, one in the drawing room. These Victorian houses were so big . . . He stood in the hallway, uncertain, looking around.

The door at the far end of the corridor was painted brown, its wood cracked and stained. It was latched, not locked. Farnsby put out a hesitant hand, unlatched the door and found himself looking down into a dark, narrow staircase. There was a light switch just inside the door. He flicked it on, light flooded into the stairs down to the cellar. He stood there for a few moments, then slowly he went down, his heels echoing on the wooden stairs.

There was little dust and no clutter in the cellar: clearly it had not been used for storage, as most cellars were, holding the unwanted detritus of yesterday's living. A boiler sighed away in the corner, providing heating for the floors above and a degree of warmth in the cellar itself. The stone walls had been boarded over, painted white. The painting was new and bright. Farnsby frowned, looked about him. There was something wrong about the dimensions of the cellar. He walked across to the wall, tapped on the board. The first two walls sounded solid enough. The third wall rang hollowly. Part of the cellar had been boarded off: a second chamber had been constructed. Farnsby inspected the boarding carefully. In the corner, its Yale lock painted over in haste, was a low, narrow door. Farnsby grimaced, considered. Then he walked back to the bottom of the steps, called up to the men above.

When they joined him he pointed to the door. 'We're going to have to force that.'

It was the work of minutes. Farnsby peered inside. The room was almost empty. It contained only a bare wooden table, a chair, and something else stacked in the corner. Farnsby walked over to the item, inspected it.

'It's a bed, isn't it, sir?'

Farnsby nodded. A small, folding bed: inside it, two blankets had been stacked. He walked back to the table, peered at it for staining. Shaking his head, he slowly walked back to the foot of the stairs, climbed out of the cellar, flicked open his mobile phone to call headquarters at Ponteland. 'We'll need a forensic team out here. Sooner rather than later.'

He shouted down to the men in the cellar, called them back upstairs. There was nothing more that they could do. They could be damaging evidence, trampling around down there.

His phone rang. It was DCI O'Connor again, his tone angry.

'These bloody mobile phone services! Farnsby, you got anything more?'

'There's a cellar,' Farnsby replied dully. 'I've called in forensics.'

He could hear O'Connor's heavy breathing. 'But the man we want isn't there . . . Farnsby, I've been thinking hard. There was someone else . . .'

'How do you mean?'

'At the Carcassonne conference. There was someone else there. He might have been told something. That means he could be the next target . . .'

3

The initial shower had eased, and Arnold was back in the pit. Dr Mwate, working industriously beside him, had come dressed for the part: his big, powerful frame was covered in a worn, shabby leather jacket, his stained jeans were tucked into heavy boots, and he wore a battered cap that had seen better days. He had said little since he arrived. He wore a preoccupied air, impervious even to Portia's flirting, seemingly wanting to concentrate on the job in hand as he worked alongside Arnold, on his knees in the pit.

They worked swiftly, aware of the threat posed by the weather. Arnold's back was aching, but the two men complemented each other well, the big Zimbabwean doing the heavier work, hoisting the baskets up the ladder to the edge of the pit where Portia received them, dragging them to one side for sifting. But it was inevitable that they would miss things, Arnold guessed, under the pressures they were facing. Even so, they came across some interesting finds as the morning wore on: pig bones, studs, a small stone that appeared to have a cross carved within a circle, two writing tablets of Roman provenance. They worked quickly, almost desperately.

'It's not the way I would recommend doing things,' Mwate muttered in a deep, grumbling tone.

Arnold agreed. But they had little choice and both men knew it. Moreover, not long after they had broken for lunch — sandwiches packed by Portia and another flask of coffee — the threats posed by the dark thunderclouds drifting in from the east became a reality. First there was a fine mist ghosting in from the sea, a wet cloak that gradually darkened the hill, shrouded the beech and oak trees, filtered down across the site towards them. Then, the breeze freshened, and the rain came — at first a light drizzle, then a steady, wind-driven downpour that made them hasten to get out of the pit, drag the tarpaulin across the mouth of the excavation, and peg it down to secure it against the gusty rain.

They sat disconsolately in the hut, staring out at the puddles accumulating around the excavated areas, sipping the last of the coffee. 'It might yet blow over,' Portia commented hopefully. She had mud up to her elbows, her jacket was wet and stained, her short black hair plastered to her scalp, and there were smears of dirt on her face.

'We'll give it an hour or so,' Karen suggested, as she washed her hands in the corner of the hut. 'In the meantime, Portia, once you've finished your coffee, you and I can get on with cleaning and sorting.' She glanced at Arnold, seated beside Dr Mwate. 'You two have been doing the heavy work. You can take a rest.'

Arnold was surprised at her consideration, though he guessed it was influenced by Mwate's presence. Julian Mwate merely nodded, hardly bothering to acknowledge the remission, staring out through the open door at the driving rain, his eyes dulled, his mood sombre. There had been an edginess to his manner all morning. He had barely spoken to Arnold or the women, and he seemed uneasy, out of sorts, showing none of his usual bonhomie. It was as though he was gripped by some kind of anxiety, dark thoughts churning in his mind. Arnold lingered over his cooling coffee, respecting Mwate's mood, as they waited in the forlorn hope of the rain easing off.

Karen and Portia were bent over the muddy pile of arte-facts on the table at the far corner of the hut, talking quietly among themselves as they inspected their finds and classified them, when Mwate growled deep in his chest, an uncertain, edgy sound. 'Brings it home to you, doesn't it?'

Arnold turned his head. 'What do you mean?'

There was a sombre look on Mwate's face. 'Death. It brings it home to you, the uncertainties of life. Especially when it's someone you know.'

Arnold was silent, not knowing how to respond. Mwate seemed to be talking almost to himself as he went on, 'It was about ten years ago that my uncle died. Back in Harare. But his death, it was a relief to our family. He had been an embarrassment for years . . . It was because of him that the family had returned to Zimbabwe.'

He was silent for a while. Then he turned his head, red-rimmed eyes staring at Arnold and yet not seeming to see him. 'I didn't feel much, when I heard he had died. And yet, when I was a child, we were close. My father and my uncle, they worked on the railway at Newcastle, and all went well enough until I was about five years old, I understand. I never did get the whole story, but my uncle, he went sort of . . . strange. He began to have visions, hallucinations . . . It was then that he took me away, to Scotland. We were in a chalet on a camping site, and it was winter and it was cold . . . he hadn't told my parents . . .'

Arnold frowned. When he had met Culpeper in the pub, the retired detective chief inspector had said something about a missing child, a distraught mother, a newspaper coverage that suggested ritual killings, and then a withdrawal, a fading away of the story . . . The family had returned to Africa.

'It caused a great deal of trouble. My mother was hysterical. She thought my uncle . . . When my father found us at the camp site, there was a terrible row. But he could not let his own brother bring trouble and disgrace to the family. That's when he decided we should return to Zim.'

'Trouble?' Arnold queried. 'What happened at the camp site?'

Mwate shrugged his heavy shoulders. 'Nothing really. My uncle had returned to the old superstitions. He tried to teach me, inculcate into me the old ways of Africa. He had never really settled in England. He'd become depressed, had strange ideas . . . it was best we went back.' Mwate's eyes cleared, the fog of memory drifting away. His eyelids seemed to flare as he stared at Arnold. 'It was from my uncle that I first heard talk of *muti*. He told me many tales up there in that cabin, stories of wonders, of men who could fly, of people who could rise from the dead . . . My father said he was a crazy man. He was bringing shame to the family by his behaviour. So we went back to Zim. And then, ten years ago, he died. And I felt nothing.'

'You said you'd been close to him as a child. But as you grew older . . .'

Mwate sighed and shook his head. 'I saw nothing of him. But the things he had told me of *muti*, they remained with me. For a while, maybe, I even believed . . . But one matures, grows away from such matters. One grows away from people. And I felt nothing when I heard he had died. My father's brother. And I felt nothing. Yet now . . .' His eyes glittered. 'It is a different matter, with Charles Midgley.'

'How do you mean?' Arnold asked after a short silence.

Mwate's dark brows were knitted in a fierce frown. 'You did not know him very well?'

'I met him only a few times. The first time, at Carcassonne.'

'Ah yes, Carcassonne.' Mwate's head swivelled so that he could stare at Arnold, his eyes intense, searching. 'He was a good man. An enthusiast. A man of principle. You did not get on well with him.'

'I wouldn't say that,' Arnold replied defensively.

'I liked Charles Midgley. I knew him well, through working with him on the committee. He could be prickly, and difficult, but he was proud of his profession, and even prouder that his amateur skills at archaeology had been recognized. He deemed it a great honour to be working with the FCAI. But he rarely held grudges, and he rarely fell out with people. But somehow, even on a brief acquaintance, you and he did not seem to get on very well.'

'I don't think—'

'What was the problem between the two of you?' Arnold hesitated. He was disinclined to answer. It was over and done with, there had been an apology, a reconciliation, it was something he did not really want to talk about.

'Was it about something that happened at Carcassonne?' Mwate demanded, his glance boring into Arnold.

'There wasn't really a problem—'

'Did he tell you something at Carcassonne, something that caused a difficulty between you?' Mwate insisted. He seemed to regard the question as important.

Arnold took a deep breath. Lamely, he said, 'It's not something I really want to talk about. I . . . well, I just made a mistake. I jumped to a conclusion which was . . . erroneous. It upset Dr Midgley, and we had a few words . . . It caused a certain coolness on his part, perhaps justifiably. But we met again later, here at Fordbridge, and it was all settled between us. It all blew over. Over and done with.'

'This mistake you mention,' Mwate queried slowly. 'What was it all about?'

Arnold shook his head, puzzled by the tension in the man's voice. 'It was a private matter between us. I think it should remain that way.'

'Even though he is now dead?'

Arnold held the man's glance. 'Maybe, especially now he's dead.'

Karen Stannard was walking towards them, brushing a lock of hair from her eyes. She stood in the open doorway, hands on hips, staring out at the rain. The afternoon was drawing on, and the dark rain clouds were still sweeping relentlessly across the sky. The tarpaulin covering the excavated pit held small pools of water and the trampled earth about was scored by rivulets trickling through the mud. 'I think we've had it,' she commented. 'It'll be dark in an hour. I can't see much point in staying on longer. I'm bushed anyway. Dr Mwate, you've done all you can. I'm very grateful for your commitment. But there's no need for you to stay longer. Arnold, there's still a bit of clearing away to do. Perhaps you wouldn't mind finishing up here, while Portia and I get back.'

'To a hot bath,' Portia called out over her shoulder, glancing provocatively at Mwate. 'I just wish I could get someone to scrub my back.'

Karen glowered at her, then looked at Arnold, raising her eyebrows in query.

'I'll clear up here,' he agreed.

Dr Julian Mwate was staring at him. He seemed oddly reluctant to leave. His mouth was grim, his glance cold, calculating. He seemed unwilling to move. Arnold was left with the impression that there was more Mwate wanted to say, questions he wanted to ask. But then, as Karen shrugged into her coat and Portia moved away from the table, he stood up, nodded. 'As you say, it will be dark soon. Our work is finished here.'

Arnold watched them go, Portia and Karen hurrying to Karen's car, Mwate trudging towards his own vehicle, head down, shoulders hunched against the driving rain, big, strong, and dissatisfied.

Arnold closed the door of the hut, and turned back to the table.

He switched on the light in the hut as he carried on working for the next two hours, setting aside pieces of material, and artefacts already cleaned, and cataloguing the small pile of items that Portia and Karen had left on the table for him to deal with. He considered phoning the pub in the nearby village, to order a meal to be ready when he had finished at the hut, but when he checked his mobile he cursed, the battery needed recharging. Outside, the rain grew in intensity, drumming on the roof of the hut, and the light faded on the hill as the wind moaned through the ill-fitting hinges of the door. At one point he thought he caught a glimpse of lights, a flash against the window, and he left the table to peer out, wondering if someone had driven up to the site. He saw nothing moving in the dim light cast from the hut windows.

Work seemed to have ceased also down at the building site. Joe Holderness's workers had cleared up and left, and Arnold glanced at his watch. It was time he himself gave up for the day. He walked over to the makeshift sink and washed his hands, removing the worst of the dirt and mud he had picked up. He was looking forward, like Portia, to a long, hot bath when he got back home. The meal would have to wait. He'd make something for himself at home.

His mind drifted back to the conversation with Julian Mwate. He wondered what had prompted the Zimbabwean to comment upon his early history, to talk of his uncle. Had it really been a reaction to the news of Charles Midgley's murder, fuelled perhaps by the guilt he was experiencing, agonizing over the death of a colleague when he admitted to having felt nothing at the death of his uncle? Arnold shook his head, puzzled. There had been something odd in Mwate's behaviour, a tension, an undercurrent of anxiety. Arnold wondered why Mwate had pressed, asking questions about the relationship between Arnold and the dead forensic scientist.

He wondered again about Carcassonne. There was the possibility that Midgley had told Mwate about the document case, and its contents — but why would Mwate seek some kind of confirmation from Arnold? Once again, he felt a stab of regret that he had not imparted the information to DCI O'Connor when he had been given the chance.

It was something he would have to remedy. He decided he would ring O'Connor when he returned to the office in the morning.

He dried his hands, shrugged into his coat, cast a last glance around the room before he switched off the light and opened the door, to step out into the darkness. The rain seemed to have slackened somewhat and moving out from the lit room into the darkness meant that it was a few moments before his eyes adjusted to the dark outside. But he suddenly realized, nevertheless, that he was not alone.

Standing some twenty feet from him, stock still in the eerie, rain-lashed darkness, was the figure of a man, big, heavy, indistinct.

'Mwate?' Arnold called out uncertainly, surmising that the big Zimbabwean had forgotten something, returned to the site. There was a brief, silent pause, and then the man came forward in a rush, crossing the distance between them in three quick strides, and at the last moment Arnold became aware of the whistling sound in the air as the club came swinging towards his head.

Instinctively he threw up one arm to protect himself, dropping to one knee as he did so. He was unable to avoid the blow entirely. It smashed into his wrist with a sickening crack and Arnold yelled aloud in shock. The power behind the blow sent him sprawling sideways and he rolled away from the door, mud and rain soaking him, splashing into the puddles growing in size around the hut. He kept rolling, still sensible enough to realize that there would be another blow coming, and he heard the harsh panting breath of the man standing above him. He looked up in the dimness, saw the arms raised and rolled again, trying desperately to scramble to his feet as a second blow came thudding down towards him.

It missed entirely, and he heard a muffled obscenity. He managed to rise to his feet, one arm hanging uselessly. He turned to run but his feet slipped in the mud and the club came hissing at him again, catching him a glancing blow across the back, and he pitched forward helplessly, splashing down again into the churned surface of the site. He turned, lay on his back, his body screaming in pain, and he was unable to move now, staring up at the man who stood above him. He raised a hand weakly, knowing it would be little or no defence against the next deadly, swinging blow aimed at his head.

But there was a dull roaring in his ears, and the sound of someone shouting. Engines gunned up the slope and the access road. Car headlights flashed on the hill, then picked out the figure of the man standing above him, outlining him, pinning him against the background darkness of the hill. Arnold caught a glimpse of a white, startled face, mouth open, breathing hard, rain plastering down the man's hair, wild, glaring eyes. There was more shouting, wheels spinning on the wet gravel of the access road, and his assailant seemed rooted to the spot, undecided, panicked. Then, as Arnold still lay there, with one protective arm raised, helpless under the prospect of another murderous blow, the voices and the trampling feet pounded nearer, and the man with the club hesitated, then turned and began to run back into the darkness.

Out of the glare of the car headlights he seemed to vanish with an inexplicable suddenness, but there was a cry, a cracking sound, the whoosh of something collapsing, and then another cry of pain. Arnold could feel nothing in his left arm, he was dizzy, struggling to lift himself by his right arm out of the mud, slipping, aware of a rolling, searing pain throughout his body. Then there was someone standing over him, taking him by the shoulder, helping him to his feet.

'Are you all right?'

Arnold tried to nod, but his senses were still whirling. He clutched at the man's slick raincoat, pulled himself upright as the shouting and the lights and the sound of feet splashing, surging about him rose crazily. There was an arm around him, supporting him, and men were yelling at each other, flashlights spinning in the darkness, sending dancing, indeterminate shadows flickering to the rain-misted hill, picking out glittering, driving rain.

'Where the hell has he gone?'

For a moment, dizzily, Arnold thought his assailant would have disappeared in the darkness, escaped, but then he heard a man call out in surprise. 'Over here, sir! Bloody hell, he's over here!'

The man supporting Arnold moved, half dragging Arnold forward across the slippery ground. Then they stood at the edge of the pit, bright beams of the flashlights directed downwards. Arnold's assailant had run off into the darkness but not knowing the site had been unlucky he had headed straight across the excavation the team had been conducting. He had stepped on to the tarpaulin, it had given way and he had gone down, crashing into the ladder which had been thrown sideways by his descent. Arnold looked down, still dazed. At his feet, on the edge of the pit, lay a baseball bat, dropped by the man in the pit.

In the pit itself he could see his assailant. He was lying on his side, clutching his knee, and groaning in pain and frustration. As Arnold stared the man turned his head, his features twisted with pain and fury, mud streaking his face. His eyes locked on Arnold's. They stared at each other for several seconds.

It was a face Arnold did not recognize. At first, stepping out into the darkness from the hut, he had thought it had been Julian Mwate, returned. But this was a face he had never consciously seen before.

'What . . . who . . .' Pain seared through his chest and he gasped. 'Who the hell is he?'

DI Farnsby leaned forward, still supporting Arnold, and grunted. 'I don't suppose you've ever seen him before. But to some, he's known as The Doctor.'

4

Assistant Chief Constable Sid Cathery rubbed his hands together in undisguised glee. His barracuda mouth was marked with vicious pleasure. His voice was thick with triumphant satisfaction. His sharp blue eyes gleamed with confident self-justification. 'Didn't I tell you guys?' he purred, leaning back in his chair and looking from one to another. 'Didn't I tell you that bastard would get his fingers into any mucky business he could? Didn't I tell you? Was I right, or was I right?'

DCI O'Connor glanced stonily at the other men in the room, DI Farnsby, flanked by DS Robinson. 'It seems you were right, sir, as you say.'

'Damn right I was,' Cathery grunted. 'You might have called it baggage I brought with me, but I call it gut instinct. I know that bastard Catford, from way back. I knew he'd be into all sorts up here. And I knew that one day I'd catch him bang to rights. So tell me now, O'Connor, tell me exactly the way it is. I want to know all the detail of what we've got on the slimy villain.'

O'Connor, still standing like the others, facing Cathery's desk, shifted his stance, folded his arms. 'We learned from Martin Woudt, when we traced him to Sainte Enimie, that the man we knew only as The Doctor was in fact Don Catford. We'd been assuming, of course, that maybe the term referred to a professional man—'

'Professional *villain*, yes,' Cathery interrupted in satisfaction. 'Doctoring cars, before shipping them off to Europe, and then into Africa and Asia. *The Doctor*. But always looking for another scam, another piece of business, any bit of filth he could get into up to his armpits.'

'That's right, sir,' DI Farnsby said woodenly. 'It seems it was Catford who set up the website, tapping into the European syndicate — which is how he came to know Martin Woudt. But he kept his identity well hidden—'

'He always was good at concealing his involvement,' Cathery admitted in a reluctant tone, rubbing a hand over his stubbly iron-grey hair. 'I'll give him that, at least.'

'But after the Starlight Club became operational he was badly shaken by two things,' O'Connor continued. 'First, there was the raid on the garage in South Shields looking for evidence of his stolen vehicle operation. He managed to cover that problem up, and initially it was just a hitch in his business dealings. But second, he lost whatever protection he'd had when . . . when senior officers in the force were asked to resign.'

'And he heard I would be coming into the manor,' Cathery insisted, a gleam of malice in his eyes. 'That must have made the bastard sit up.'

'I think that also had something to do with it,' O'Connor agreed, unable to keep the reluctance out of his tone. Cathery looked at him. He was aware O'Connor disliked his triumphalism, but he cared nothing for that — his day had come.

'Anyway,' O'Connor continued, 'Catford slowed down for a while, moved the car doctoring business, but then hit another rock.' He glanced at DS Robinson.

The burly detective sergeant ducked his head in acknowledgement. 'The Starlight Club. Catford had covered his tracks well in setting up the ring, but there was always the chance we'd find him, work out his identity. So he was running scared.'

'Panicked, in fact,' O'Connor agreed. 'That's when he realized it was too dangerous to go forward with the next step he'd set up with Dr Martin Woudt.'

'Which was?' Cathery asked.

There was a sour taste on O'Connor's tongue. 'A step beyond merely providing pornographic images over the Internet. Giving members the real thing. Providing children, for the use of members of the Starlight Club.'

There was a short silence. Cathery glowered in distaste at O'Connor. 'Go on.'

'Woudt had suggested to him that now the Starlight Club was up and running, he would be able to provide through the European network, untraceable children for . . . the use of the members. Catford agreed, there'd be big money in it. So the deal was made, Woudt smuggled in a boy, the child of illegal African immigrants, brought him to Catford . . .'

'We raided an address Woudt gave us, a house of Catford's, in Gosforth,' Farnsby interrupted. 'We think we'll get forensic evidence from the cellar. It was where the boy was kept, briefly.'

'Briefly?' Cathery enquired.

'The scheme never really got off the ground,' O'Connor explained. 'The boy was smuggled in, but his . . . availability was never even made known on the website, because we'd started our arrests, Catford felt he was under our eye over the car doctoring, and he decided the game wasn't on.'

'So he just got rid of the boy,' Cathery said slowly.

O'Connor managed, a diffident shrug. 'The child was an embarrassment. What would have been a lucrative business had turned sour, it was too dangerous, Catford felt too exposed. The boy had to disappear.'

Cathery fixed O'Connor with a contemplative stare. 'You been getting all this from Woudt? I can't see Catford holding up his hands and saying it was a fair cop.'

'When we bounced Woudt a bit in Sainte Enimie he gave up the ghost. Catford had told Woudt merely that he would not proceed with the new arrangement, once the Starlight Club was closed down, and he would solve the problem of the child. Woudt wanted to know no more about it, didn't discuss how Catford would get rid of the boy . . . but he began to worry when he heard about the discovery of the torso in the Tyne. He discussed it with Midgley, apparently, but was relieved to find we had no clues as to the child's identity. But he still asked no questions of Catford, didn't want to know . . .'

Farnsby shuffled impatiently. 'Martin Woudt is talking loudly enough now, because he doesn't want to be nailed on a murder charge. He's admitting membership of the European network of sickos, and he's even admitted smuggling the sedated child into the country in the boot of his car. But the killing of the child, and what went on afterwards . . . he wants nothing to do with that, scared that he might personally be saddled with the killing. As a result, he's fingered Catford.'

'So it was my old friend Catford who killed the boy,' Cathery ruminated with a subdued glee that seemed inappropriate in the discussion.

'Dismembered him to prevent identification, and buried body parts at Seaton Sluice before dumping the torso into the sea, where it washed up into the Tyne at high tide. We were side-tracked by the *muti* theory,' O'Connor admitted. 'It was all about identification, right from the beginning.'

The horrific images the comments presented silenced the whole group for a while. Some of Cathery's triumphalism had died away. He linked his fingers together, twisted his hands in disgust. 'All right, so how does the rest link in?'

O'Connor shrugged. 'It could have stopped there, as far as Catford was concerned. He'd concealed his identity as The Doctor, he'd removed a potential danger with the disposal of the boy, and there was no way Woudt would be talking to the police or anyone else, in view of his own culpability. They could wait, let things calm down, and then get on with life.'

'But . . . ?'

'But we put more pressure on Catford . . .' O'Connor hesitated. 'That was your idea, sir, but as it happened it was turning an already tight screw. Because in the meanwhile Martin Woudt had made a bad mistake. At a conference in Carcassonne he was stupid enough to have carried some pornographic photographs with him. They came to the attention of Charles Midgley. He guessed they belonged to Woudt, by a process of elimination. He faced Woudt, told him such activity would bring discredit upon the FCAI. Told him he'd have to resign from the committee, and from the Rijksmuseum, or face exposure. Midgley was not prepared to have the FCAI . . . dishonoured, as he saw it. Woudt told Catford he had to comply. Catford immediately saw the danger. Midgley might have promised Woudt he'd keep his mouth shut if Woudt resigned, but there was too much at stake. Midgley might still talk about Woudt's inclinations, the rumours could spread, the whole thing could be revealed. Including what had happened to the boy . . . Catford is a blunt instrument. He could see only one sensible way forward. Remove Midgley from the equation.'

'He got Woudt to set up the meeting at Newcastle airport?' Cathery asked.

'Woudt denies that, but it's highly likely. And Woudt must have known what was about to happen. That's why he not only resigned from the FCAI, but he went to ground, using his old name of Steiner, hiding out at Sainte Enimie. Not just from us — from Catford too, probably. Things were getting out of hand, with Catford on the rampage.' O'Connor paused. 'We have Inspector Garcia to thank for the trace. And when we confronted Woudt, and he realized how much we already knew, and seemed committed to putting him in the frame, he squealed like a stuck pig.'

'So Catford, *The Doctor*, killed the boy, and then Midgley, to cover his tracks. And, in time, he would probably have had a go at Woudt too,' Cathery considered thoughtfully.

'Woudt certainly thought it a possibility,' O'Connor agreed. 'But then, once Woudt started talking, and we made the link with Midgley, it raised another possibility. Woudt had told Catford how Midgley came to discover his involvement with pornography, at the conference in Carcassonne.

A moment's carelessness, that's how he described it, carrying the photographs in his document case. But the document case had been handed to Midgley by Arnold Landon, and Midgley had been to see Landon at the Fordbridge site, the morning before Midgley made his way for his appointment with Woudt at Newcastle airport—'

'Only to be met by Catford,' Farnsby added. 'So Catford knew it was possible Midgley might have let slip something to Landon. It meant Landon also could be a danger . . . DCI O'Connor phoned me from Sainte Enimie, told me to get hold of Landon, reach him before Catford did. We now know Catford had been watching Landon, waiting his moment. That moment came out at the Fordbridge site, when Landon was alone. We'd tried Landon's office, discovered he was at Fordbridge, tried phoning him on his mobile to warn him, but couldn't get through, so we were forced to drive out there. But we managed to get there just in time . . .'

Sid Cathery rubbed his hands again, washing them vigorously in obvious satisfaction. 'The chief constable will be pleased. It means we've cleared up the Starlight Club, the killing of the boy, and the murder of Charles Midgley. And we've got the perpetrator bang to rights.' His brow furrowed suddenly. 'Do we know who the boy was?'

O'Connor shook his head. 'Inspector Garcia suggests we never will trace his identity. An immigrant family, probably illegals, they might even have sold the kid to Woudt. He thinks we have no chance.'

'So the bloody dismemberment probably wasn't even necessary.' Cathery grunted in disgust. 'And that other character . . . George Baggs?'

'We won't be proceeding further,' O'Connor replied stiffly. 'Charges dropped. Garcia tells me they now have an arrest for the killing of the girl in the Netherlands, and the Finnish student found in the Rhine. A Russian truck driver. No connection with Baggs. So we've let Baggs go. We've told him to keep his fists to himself, and advised him to stay away from Jeannette Bartoli.'

'He's already gone back to live with her, apparently,' DS Robinson advised.

Cathery grunted. 'Some people you can't help. However . . . decks cleared, it seems. Operation Headhunter successfully concluded. You lads . . .' He looked them over appraisingly, pleased with himself. 'You haven't done badly. Slates are wiped clean. A good start. I get the feeling that under my guidance, you guys will make a good team yet.'

O'Connor remained unconvinced. And he guessed from the silence of his colleagues in the room that none of them reciprocated Sid Cathery's views.

* * *

On his first day back at work, Arnold was called into Karen Stannard's office. Both Portia Tyrrel and Dr Julian Mwate were there. Karen eyed him as he entered, motioned him to take a seat. 'How are you feeling?'

'Bored, and ready to come back to work,' Arnold replied.

'Your wrist?'

'It was broken, but it's set and the plaster should be coming off in a week or so.'

'Your ribs?'

'They're okay.' He did not mention the occasional searing pain he suffered when he forgot about the injury and twisted his upper body. In time it would ease, he knew.

'We've just been talking about the work at Fordbridge.' Karen advised him. 'We've had to close down, for the time being. But Dr Mwate informs us that the FCAI will be holding to their financial promises.'

'And Karen will indeed be joining the committee,' Mwate added, 'while I'll take over FCAI supervision of the site.' He hesitated, uncertainly, his eyes narrowed as he looked at Arnold. 'It'll be good to see you back at work. And it's good to see you getting fit.' He shifted in his chair, uneasily. 'The man who attacked you . . . I still wonder whether I might have been next on his list.'

Arnold raised his eyebrows. 'You? Why?'

'As far as I can gather, this man Catford was trying to silence anyone who might have . . . talked with Charles Midgley about what happened at Carcassonne.'

'Had Dr Midgley talked to you about the document case?' Arnold queried, surprised.

Mwate shook his heavy head. 'No, not really. But I knew there was something up. It's why I was asking you up at the site that day . . . It was all so odd. I knew something had gone wrong at Carcassonne: Midgley upset with you, Woudt resigning so suddenly . . . I did ask Midgley what was going on, but he told me it was better I didn't know.'

'He was very protective of the FCAI reputation,' Karen murmured.

Arnold nodded. 'It cost him his life.'

In the short silence that followed Dr Julian Mwate stood up. 'Yes, well, it's all over now. A bad business . . . but I must be going. We'll see more of each other, I'm sure.'

'Count on it,' Portia Tyrrel replied demurely, never willing to lose an opportunity. 'I'll see you to your car, Dr Mwate.'

After she had led the way from the room Karen Stannard regarded Arnold with dark, quizzical eyes. 'In a way, the FCAI almost cost you your life, also.'

'I don't see that.'

'I asked you to come to Carcassonne to try to help get FCAI support for Fordbridge. If you hadn't been there, you wouldn't have been the one who triggered these events.' She paused, contemplatively. 'And you wouldn't have been attacked by Catford, in the darkness.'

'It's all behind us now,' Arnold replied.

'All behind us, yes.' Her eyes suddenly seemed very green as her glance held his for a long moment. 'But who knows what the future might hold?'

There was a hint of promise in her glance, but Arnold had never placed much store in Karen Stannard's promises.

THE END

Thank you for reading this book.

If you enjoyed it please leave feedback on Amazon or Goodreads, and if there is anything we missed or you have a question about, then please get in touch. We appreciate you choosing our book.

Founded in 2014 in Shoreditch, London, we at Joffe Books pride ourselves on our history of innovative publishing. We were thrilled to be shortlisted for Independent Publisher of the Year at the British Book Awards.

www.joffebooks.com

We're very grateful to eagle-eyed readers who take the time to contact us. Please send any errors you find to corrections@joffebooks.com. We'll get them fixed ASAP.